Pursuing Happiness

Humanities-Ebooks Genre Fiction Monographs
Series Editor: John Lennard

Pursuing Happiness
Reading American Romance
as Political Fiction

Laura Vivanco

HEB ☼ Humanities-Ebooks

Copyright

First published by *Humanities-Ebooks LLP*,
Tirril Hall, Tirril, Penrith CA10 2JE.

This PDF ebook is available from http://www.humanities-ebooks.
co.uk and to libraries from Ebrary, EBSCO and Ingram. A Kindle
ebook is available from Amazon. but the PDF is recommended for
its superior performance on devices larger than cellphones.

A paperback is available from Lulu.com and from all booksellers.

The author and publisher have used their best efforts to ensure that
external URLs given in this book are accurate and current. They are
not, however, responsible for any of the websites, and can offer no
guarantee that the sites remain live or the content appropriate.

ISBN 978-1-84760-359-3 PDF
ISBN 978-1-84760-360-9 Paperback
ISBN 978-1-84760-361-6 Kindle
ISBN 978-1-84760-362-3 ePub

"'We hold these truths to be self-evident,'" Savannah said, reciting the Declaration of Independence to the class-room, "'that all men are created equal ...'"

She paused here, as an image of Jake popped into her mind. *Equal, yes*, she thought, *but certainly not the same*. She'd never met a more virile man than Jake.

Realizing the children were staring at her, she blinked back to the present and continued, "'that they are endowed"

Good grief, yes, he most certainly—'"

Stop that! She frowned and shook the thought from her mind.

"'... by their creator,'" she moved on, "'with certain inalienable rights, that among these are life, liberty and the pursuit of happiness.'"

The pursuit of happiness.

—Barbara McCauley, *Texas Heat*

To Monica Jackson
(1959–2012)

and

Liz Montgomery
(1967–2015)

Contents

List of Illustrations

Cover Image: "Grunge textured flag of the United States on vintage paper, with 50 hearts instead of stars", by Nicolas Raymond. Made available for use at <http://freestock.ca/flags_maps_g80-us_love_grunge_flag_p1095.html> under a Creative Commons Attribution 3.0 Unported License.

Page 24: "Extase" (1991 / Cryo Interactive / Atari ST). Courtesy of Daniel Rehn. Available at <https://www.flickr.com/photos/daniel-rehn/9318371465/> under a Creative Commons 2.0 Generic licence <https://creativecommons.org/licenses/by/2.0/>.

Page 44: "Workers" road sign from "Part 6—Temporary Traffic Control" of the Federal Highway Administration's *Manual on Uniform Traffic Control Devices* (2009; rev. 2012). <http://mutcd.fhwa.dot.gov/pdfs/2009r1r2/part6.pdf>.

Page 62: A "prairie schooner". Released into the public domain and donated to the Wikimedia Foundation by the Archives of Pearson Scott Foresman. <https://commons.wikimedia.org/wiki/File:Prairie_schooner_%28PSF%29.png>.

Page 88: The Statue of Liberty. Photographed by João Carlos Medau on 11 February 2014. Online at flickr <https://www.flickr.com/photos/medau/13365028933> under a Creative Commons 2.0 generic licence.

Page 110: "Tumbleweeds lodged against a Wire Fence in Winter" from Joseph Y. Bergen's *Foundations of Botany* (Boston: Ginn & Company, 1901). Internet Archive: at <https://archive.org/stream/foundationsofbot00bergrich#page/380/mode/2up>.

Preface

This book is dedicated to Monica Jackson and to Liz Montgomery. Monica Jackson (1959–2012) was a romance author who kept asking:

> why black racial separation is so prevalent in romance. My favorite theory is that it's the nature of the romance genre. Romance is fantasy-based. Readers are notoriously picky about their settings and having sympathetic characters that they can relate to [...]. These are a few of the reasons, but figuring out how to address the issue of segregation in romance and thinking about how to go about changing it, is a daunting task. Race is an uncomfortable and taboo subject to discuss on nearly any level by almost anybody, black or white. Desegregating any institution in this country has always been a monumental struggle.

Her courage and persistence in speaking out about the racial politics of romance fiction inspired and motivated me.

Liz Montgomery (1967–2015) was a romance reader and reviewer whom I knew as "Meoskop". Never content to just 'say something nice', she "bang[ed] on a lot about the way domestic violence can be subtly normalized in the genre" and critiqued the "strong pressure in the genre to suppress personal emotions for socially prescribed reasons" which led to the production of "characters [who] are saintly".

That said, she loved romance fiction and once wrote that:

> My path is to take the core message of romance, that we all deserve happy endings, and live it in my daily life. I don't want to see your academic or social qualifications. They don't matter to me. You do. Because you are enough, as you are, without any external validation. You spent the most precious commodity any of us have, our limited time in this life, on experiencing a piece of art.

Monica and Liz's time in life was limited, their endings came too soon; I'm grateful for the ways in which they shared their "most precious commodity" with their fellow romance readers.

I would also like to thank British romance author Joanna Chambers. Some years ago she gave me her copy of LaVyrle Spencer's *Morning Glory* and challenged me to explain its appeal to American romance readers. That was the seed from which this book grew.

Acknowledgments

The quotation from Monica Jackson in the above Preface is from
http://www.likesbooks.com/209.html
Liz Montgomery quotations in the above Preface are from:
http://www.vivanco.me.uk/blog/post/being-admirable-repressing-complaint
http://loveinthemargins.com/2014/02/09/is-it-romance-or-is-it-erotica/
http://loveinthemargins.com/2014/02/23/moonstruck-madness-and-domestic-violence/
http://loveinthemargins.com/2014/10/23/class-and-privilege-the-listen-linda-edition/

Introduction

AMERICAN popular culture is "big business"; its wide appeal ensures that what it is "saying about and to Americans everywhere is important" (E. Richards 19). Some individual creators of popular works, like Travis Hagen, the comic-artist hero of Emilie Richards's 1985 romance novel *Gilding the Lily*, may of course demur, arguing that they had "no idea" their output "would be considered social commentary by anyone. I make it a point to stay away from politics and religion" (19). However, as romance heroine and scholar of popular culture Lesley Belmont retorts, "We both know that's not true [...] they're rife with political comment. They're just very subtle. The message is even more far-reaching that way, I'll bet" (19).

It has long been recognised that one may do worse than study popular culture if one wishes to understand a society and its attitudes. A tourist in early nineteenth-century England who chose to consult the *Leeds Guide; Including a Sketch of the Environs, and Kirkstall Abbey* would have been informed that:

> Public amusements, especially those of the Drama are calculated to give us an insight into the taste and manners of a nation; in popular Tragedies, we trace the refinement of the passions; Comedies are often satires on existing follies and fashions of the times; and even Pantomimes generally exhibit caricatures of the frivolities of the day. (Ryley 61)

More recently, Ray B. Browne, a pioneer of popular-culture studies, declared that "the popular culture of a country is the voice of the people—their likes and dislikes, the lifeblood of daily existence, their way of life" (1). This book explores what one form of US popular culture, its romance fiction, reveals about Americans' political "likes and dislikes". (The Americas include, but extend far beyond, the USA. However, since the focus of this book is on the USA, unless specified otherwise the word "American" is used here to refer specifically to people, places, etc from the USA.)

Romance novels have often been described as "escapist" but romance readers cannot escape politics because:

> Politics is everywhere. This is so because no realm of life is immune to relations of conflict and power. There is always the possibility that social relations could be ordered differently, which means that there is inevitable dispute as to the most appropriate, or just, way of organizing these relations otherwise. (Squires 119)

At the most basic level, there is bound to be politics in romance fiction because the love lives of the two or more protagonists in a romance will invariably involve "relations of conflict and power". There is, moreover, no way of wholly separating the private sphere from the public when the latter so often influences the former. In many of Jayne Ann Krentz's romances, for example:

> the hero and heroine are initially constructed as "good" at work and "bad" at love, yet they both ultimately become part of a successful and contented romantic couple due to their transference of management skills and business ethics into the relationship. (Young 97)

Applying some of the terminology and practices of the workplace to marriage is nothing new: the early twentieth century saw a "remarkable infusion of business language into the sphere once held apart for love and sentiment" (Rodgers 200). This was a period in which the:

> *Ladies' Home Journal* [...] ridiculed the idea of working wives [...] but [...] held up a model of the middle-class woman as a business partner in her husband's success, doing her share by maintaining an efficiently managed home. [...] Even marriage could be put into the language of work; it was a matter of persistence, industry, and patience—woman's "specific share of the world's work." (Rodgers 200)

Although much has changed in the intervening decades, "the

'marriage as work' formula" (Celello 2) has persisted and thrived to such an extent that now "The pairing of 'marriage' and 'work' is so pervasive and reflexive that it is difficult to imagine a time in which this was not a guiding maxim of American unions" (Celello 1–2).

The writing of novels which depict these unions is also a form of work and is shaped by economic factors. Romances are a type of popular fiction and as such can be considered:

> commodities that are typically developed in accordance with mainstream convictions—[…] in capitalism as the ideal economic system, in wars fought in the name of democracy, and in heterosexuality and whiteness as the normative state for romantic experience. (Kamblé 23)

In my conclusion, I explore some of the "mainstream convictions" present in the work of LaVyrle Spencer, who has been described as "the classic, quintessential romance writer, whose novels are regularly reprinted and kept in stock" (Chappel 108), and in particular her *Morning Glory* (1989), which won the Romance Writers of America's award for "Best Romance of 1989" and was made into a movie, released in 1993, starring Christopher Reeve and Deborah Raffin.

Explicitly political statements and, indeed, explicitly American political statements, can be found in US romance novels, including Lynna Banning's *Smoke River Bride* (2013):

> "But this is America," she shouted in the strongest voice she had ever used. "We are all kinds of people, with all kinds of backgrounds. We all have the same rights because that is what this country stands for." (229)

Despite the fact that, as Banning acknowledged in a note placed at the beginning of this novel, "As a nation, we have not always shown tolerance toward those who are 'different' from us" (6), her romance's half-Chinese heroine seeks to counter racial discrimination by portraying it as un-American; the reference to "the same rights" would seem to allude to the Declaration of Independence's famous assertion "that all men are created equal, that they are endowed by their Creator with certain unalienable Rights".

Authors who choose to include explicitly political statements in their works do risk being unpopular with readers, who may find themselves in disagreement or simply "feel that political education spoils a good romance" (Hermes 51). In general, therefore, the politics in romance remains implicit and may not be obvious to readers of mainstream romances who themselves feel part of the mainstream: for them, the politics in the novels may well go unperceived because it reaffirms widely accepted political beliefs. For instance, when the heroine of Justine Davis's *Deadly Temptation* (2007) declares that:

> she was all for free enterprise, but stealing someone else's work wasn't her idea of the way things were supposed to be. It had been ingrained in her from childhood by her father; you were supposed to use your own talents and skills, make it on your own merit, not rob from others. There was no satisfaction, no pride to be found in success you hadn't earned. (152–3)

readers may simply accept this as a passage which describes the values of the heroine and her family, rather than reading the passage as an encapsulation of the essence of the American Dream blended with the American Work Ethic.

Given the core plot of romance novels, however, even readers who generally shy away from the overtly political, and who overlook much of the implicit politics in romance novels, may find it impossible to avoid noticing the fact that romances deal with gender and sexual politics. Indeed, they may actively appreciate romances for offering a vision of better "social relations" between the sexes. The readers interviewed by Janice A. Radway in her influential study, undertaken in 1980–81, for instance, were mostly "married mothers of children, living in single-family homes in a sprawling suburb of a central midwestern state" (50) and:

> They made it clear [...] that they believe their self-perception has been favorably transformed by their reading. [...] Although marriage is still the idealized goal in all of the novels they like best, that marriage is always characterized by the male partner's recognition and appreciation of the heroine's

saucy assertion of her right to defy outmoded conventions and manners. This fiction encourages them to believe that marriage and motherhood do not necessarily lead to loss of independence or identity. (102)

For other readers, however, the gender and sexual politics, or indeed other aspects of the implicit politics, of mainstream romances can be distinctly unpalatable. Such readers may therefore seek out specific authors or sub-genres in which the politics is more in line with their own beliefs.

An "idealized goal" of heterosexual marriage, for example, reflects a political context which is at best heteronormative, at worst homophobic, and would have been unachievable by the lesbian readers of lesbian romance novels surveyed by Jill Ehnenn in the 1990s, of whom:

only half [...] were able to report that their work/home environment was "pretty accepting" as opposed to "kind of" or "very" homophobic. It seems that reading for escape and reading as affirmation might often be related for lesbians who read in order to escape from an environment that makes them feel negatively about their sexual identity. (124)

For very different reasons, many evangelical Christian readers also prefer novels which offer an alternative to the "social relations" depicted in secular romances of the kind read by Radway's interviewees: they "want stories that, unlike secular romances, affirm their spiritual ideals and offer wholesome entertainment" (Neal 78).

When seeking to understand American politics in the broadest sense, romance novels written by Americans and sold in the US provide "an excellent form of evidence because they have a large and dedicated readership (41 million readers in 1998, 51.1 million in 2002) of, in many ways, statistically average American women" (Clawson 462). Despite the disdain and suspicion which has often been directed at it, romance has been described as "the dominant form of American fiction" (Regis, "Female" 847) and in the years since 1960, when the Romantic Novelists' Association (RNA) was founded in the UK, "the geographic center of romance writing and publishing has shifted from Great Britain and the Commonwealth to North America" (Mussell 8).

In parallel with this shift, the composition of the RNA has altered:

> In the beginning the members were mostly 'romance' writers—that is, short books dealing mainly with one-on-one relationships and with small canvasses. Now we cover an enormous range of women's fiction from Mills & Boon [or Harlequins, as they are known in the US] through to operatic-sized epics, taking in on the way, sagas, chick-lit, contemporary situation novels [...], historicals, paranormal, and whatever the next fashion is going to be. (Haddon and Pearson 9)

Yet, even allowing for these broader parameters, romantic fiction in the UK would appear to be in decline. Joanna Trollope, in an address given to the RNA's fiftieth anniversary conference in July 2010, took stock of its "present state" in the UK and told her fellow romantic novelists that when she had:

> looked at the *Sunday Times* bestseller lists this morning [...] in the hardback fiction top ten, there are six crime or thriller novels, and in the paperback list, there are another six. That's twelve of a single genre out of twenty. Romantic fiction has four out of twenty [...]. It isn't selling in the quantities that it could, or even deserves, to sell. (Haddon and Pearson 256–7)

By contrast, in the US that same month, *Bloomberg Businessweek* reported that romance was "the top-performing category on the best-seller lists compiled by *The New York Times*, *USA Today*, and industry trade *Publishers Weekly*". This success is very far from being a temporary aberration: "In 1999, for example, more than 2,500 romances were published in North America, accounting for 55.9 percent of mass market and trade paperbacks sold" (Regis, "Female" 847).

There is, however, a significant difference between US popular romance fiction, which comes with the guarantee of an "emotionally-satisfying and optimistic ending" (Romance Writers of America), and the UK's 'romantic fiction', which offers readers a range of outcomes. This US bias towards happy endings is not limited to romance novels: it has been observed that "the centrality and significance of the happy ending in American popular culture contrasts sharply with the endings offered in many European-produced works" (Crothers 45). It might therefore be reasonable to speculate that the differences in the endings of these works of fiction reflect differing cultural and political beliefs. Certainly, in depicting their protagonists' journey towards happiness, romance novels often reproduce a narrative which, according to Dan McAdams, an American psychologist, "provides Americans of many different persuasions with a common language or format for making sense of an individual life": the story of the "redemptive self" ("American" 20).

An American who understands the events in their own life in terms of this narrative will tend to feel they were "chosen for a special status" due to possessing "some kind of physical, mental, psychological, social, economic, ideological, or spiritual advantage" (McAdams, "The Redemptive" 91); the heroes and heroines of a romance novel are ascribed "a special status" by virtue of being chosen as the protagonists of the novels in which they appear but it is also common for them to be special in some way compared to other characters and, indeed, the reader (Vivanco 29–37). As the non-fictional life-story continues, the narrator will recount how:

> As I move forward in life, many bad things come my way—sin, sickness, abuse, addiction, injustice, poverty, stagnation. But bad things often lead to good outcomes—my suffering is redeemed. Redemption comes to me in the form of atonement, recovery, emancipation, enlightenment, upward social mobility, and/or the actualization of my good inner self. As the plot unfolds, I continue to grow and progress. I bear fruit; I give back; I offer a unique contribution. I will make a happy ending, even in a threatening world. (McAdam "American" 20)

Similarly, popular romance novels can be considered texts in which:

> the shared and underlying mythic conviction is in the idealizing power of love to make the world, in reality so often harsh and even tragic, a better place. In line with the promise of orthodox religious faith, love offers the promise of redemption

and even salvation. (Roach)

Pamela Regis, an American romance scholar, has observed that two essential elements of the romance novel must be endured and overcome before the protagonists can achieve happiness. These are a "barrier" which prevents the immediate union of the protagonists and can take the form of "any psychological vice, virtue, or problem, any circumstance of life, whether economic, geographical, or familial" (*A Natural* 32), and a:

> "point of ritual death" [...] marked by death or its simulacrum (for example fainting or illness); by the risk of death; or by any number of images or events that suggest death, however metaphorically (for example, darkness, sadness, despair, or winter). (14)

In Pamela Browning's *Feathers in the Wind* (1989), for example, the heroine, Caro, suffers a violent attack which leaves her with a "scar stretching in a dark jagged line from her right ear to her lower left jaw" (12) and, more importantly, with psychological scars that hinder the development of her relationship with the hero. Caro's is "a story of survival" (223) which she believes could "inspire people, make them want to go on against all the odds" (223); it demonstrates "that sometimes you have to go through the bad part of life to get to the good" (236).

Romances, then, like the real-life "redemptive narratives" studied by McAdams:

> are not simply happy stories. Rather, they are stories of suffering and negativity that turn positive in the end. Without the negative emotions, there can be no redemption in the story. (McAdams, *Redemptive* 44)

McAdams argues that such stories draw on "images, themes, characters, plots, and scenes that resonate with some of the most cherished and contested narratives in the American heritage" (McAdams, "American" 26), including "'rags-to-riches' stories about 'the American dream' [...] along with transformative stories about being 'born again,' [and] 'escaping from slavery to freedom'"

(McAdams, "The Redemptive" 82). As fictional redemption narratives, many American romance novels surely recall them too.

The underlying optimism of such texts would seem to set them apart from much modern 'literary' or 'serious' fiction which, perhaps not coincidentally, "has long been subsidized by mass-market fiction and by nonfiction ripped from the headlines" (Donadio):

> Love, success, and many displaced mythic oppositions between good America and evil others no longer grip readers and writers of serious fiction [...], the traditional literary themes and structures have lost appeal in part because so many Americans have lost faith in America's future, in America's righteousness, and in the power, meaning, and integrity of the individual. (Hume 5–6)

One can, however, continue to find "faith in America's future, in America's righteousness, and in the power, meaning, and integrity of the individual" expressed in popular romance novels. Indeed, for many years the guidelines for Harlequin's line of American Romance novels quite explicitly stated that these novels should demonstrate "a sense of adventure, optimism and a lively spirit—they're all the best of what it means to be American!" (Harlequin).

According to the Founding Fathers, being American meant being a citizen of a country in which it was believed "that all men are created equal, that they are endowed by their Creator with certain unalienable Rights, that among these are Life, Liberty and the pursuit of Happiness". In practice the US has not always lived up to its high ideals but for the romance authors who acknowledge that fact in their work, this would not seem to justify despair or apathy. Instead the underlying themes of their novels can be encapsulated in the words of a secondary character in Nell Stark's *Homecoming* (2008):

> Liberty and justice for all. I believe in that, and I know you do, too. I believe that the United States has a good system— imperfect, but good. I believe that we are doing exactly the right thing—exposing and working to change the parts of that system that are weak. (194)

Some of the imperfections of the system are revealed via the stories of the African-American hero and heroine of Beverly Jenkins's *Belle* (2002) and the lesbian protagonists of Karin Kallmaker's *In Every Port* (1989), all of whom make an appearance in Chapter 4. These novels bear witness to the struggles of various minority groups to make it truly self-evident to US society as a whole that "all men are created equal". The task of "exposing and working to change the parts of that system that are weak" is also shouldered by the novels in Nora Roberts's MacKade series (1995–6) and Sharon Shinn's Twelve Houses series (2005–8) which literally and metaphorically attempt to set houses in order and can therefore be read as blueprints for how to create better, stronger communities.

Pamela Morsi's *Simple Jess* (1996) is the subject of Chapter 2 and a novel which suggests that a man's status in his community owes a great deal to his ability to work, and the type of work he is able to perform. There is a broad consensus in the US that "In America hard work leads to good fortune which in turn results in money/fame/ power for the virtuous individual" (Nachbar and Lause 95). This American work ethic may be deemed to set the US apart from other countries. That is certainly the opinion of the foreign-born hero of Kate Welsh's *A Texan's Honour* (2012), who decided to make his home in the US because of Americans':

> integrity in choosing honest work and self-determined prosperity over inherited wealth and idleness [...]. And nowhere on the continent did that quality hold stronger and truer than what he'd found when he'd visited and fallen in love with Texas. (90)

In Chapter 3 I too go west, in order to explore the significance of the West in the American political imagination.

The depiction of the West in some romances appears to have been influenced by "the frontier thesis advanced by Frederick Jackson Turner" at the end of the nineteenth century, a thesis which "captivated the discipline of American history for four decades" and presented the West as "a sociocultural furnace that forged a new Americanism embodying democracy, individualism, pragmatism, and a healthy nationalism" (Malone 410). By contrast, a more recent generation of historians known as:

> the new western historians set aside the mythic history of
> the pioneer and national innocence that underlay Turnerian
> histories in favor of a more critical assessment of expansion.
> For the new western historians, the West was, and remains, a
> complex and contested place filled with diverse peoples and
> stamped by the mark of conquest. (Smoak 86)

This approach, too, finds its counterpart in romance fiction. In Chapter
3 I show how Ruth Jean Dale's *Legend!* (1993) and Ruth Wind's
Meant to be Married (1998) reassess Western history and critique its
violence. The past continues to affect the present; historic violence
and discrimination shape contemporary Americans' narratives about
their "roots", as I shall show in Chapter 5.

   Conflict is also discussed in Chapter 1. Here, though, the primary
struggle is between the literary critic and the author. In Chapter 1 I
discuss authorial intent and the limits of a critic's expertise in the
context of Linnea Sinclair's *Games of Command* (2007). One might
say that, by way of a discussion of her treatment of gender politics, I
address the politics of literary criticism.

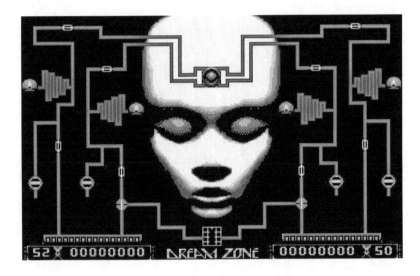

Extase

Image of Extase (1991 / Cryo Interactive / Atari ST) "Each level represented a different level of emotion until the final extase (ecstasy)."

1. Games of Command: The Politics of Literary Criticism

'When *I* use a word,' Humpty Dumpty said, in rather a scornful tone, 'it means just what I choose it to mean—neither more nor less.'

'The question is,' said Alice, 'whether you *can* make words mean so many different things.'

'The question is,' said Humpty Dumpty, 'which is to be master—that's all.' [...]

'You seem very clever at explaining words, Sir,' said Alice. 'Would you kindly tell me the meaning of the poem called "Jabberwocky"?'

'Let's hear it,' said Humpty Dumpty. 'I can explain all the poems that ever were invented—and a good many that haven't been invented just yet.' —Lewis Carroll, *Through the Looking Glass* (190–1)

One of the most serious charges that can be laid against literary critics is that we take command of literary texts, appropriating them and insisting they mean what we want them to mean regardless of whether or not our criticism "grow[s] out of the art it deals with" (Frye 6). Sadly it has to be admitted that in our approach to texts some of us probably do bear too close a resemblance to the character I think of as 'Professor Dumpty'. He is, of course, a comical creation but, as science fiction romance author Linnea Sinclair discovered, the situation may suddenly become rather less amusing if you are the author of a text to which he, or someone like him, might turn his attention:

Eons ago, when I was in college (or it might have been grad school), I remember listening to a professor expounded [sic] on what L. Frank Baum really meant to say when he wrote the

[sic] *Wizard of Oz*. It had something to do with repressed homosexual urges and a fascination with bestiality ... well, you
can figure out the rest. It was, to my way of thinking, really
off the wall. And of course, L. Frank was dead and couldn't
walk up to the professor and pop the man one in the eye for
his far-fetched statements.

But the prof said all this with such authority. Because he
was a learned prof and therefore, knew more than the poor
little author did.

I laughed about it then. Being a poor little author myself,
I'm not laughing about it now. [...] Point is this [...]: ask me.
Ask any author why they wrote the book they did, why their
characters are such, why the plot took the twist it did. [...] Ask.
("Debunking")

I came across Sinclair's post as I started to do some background
research on one of her novels, *Games of Command* (2007); I thought
I'd spotted some similarities between it and L. Frank Baum's *The
Wizard of Oz* (1900).

In both novels the action really begins when the protagonists
encounter a powerful natural phenomenon: in Baum's novel it is a
cyclone and in Sinclair's romance a "vortex—a hole violently torn in
the space-time continuum" (20). Admittedly the spaceship inhabited
by Sinclair's characters isn't immediately transported to another
dimension by the vortex, but I consoled myself with the thought that
it could have been: by the end of the novel Admiral Branden Kel-
Paten has proven his hypothesis "that we can use a vortex as a form
of intergalactic travel. Faster than the jumpdrives we currently have
and without the need for jumpgate technology" (122). Both novels
feature a diminutive female protagonist who has an even smaller
pet. Dorothy, in *The Wizard of Oz*, is "a little girl" (5); her animal
companion is Toto, "a little black dog, with long silky hair and small
black eyes that twinkled merrily on either side of his funny, wee nose.
Toto played all day long, and Dorothy [...] loved him dearly" (2).
Captain Tasha "Sass" Sebastian is certainly not a child but she is a
"pint-size female" (8), and Tank is "her furzel. Fidget, really, as he
was not yet full grown. A ten-pound fluffy bundle of long black and

white fur with an unstoppable curiosity, an insatiable appetite, and a heart full of unconditional love" (4). Like Toto, who is prepared to defend his mistress against attack by a lion, Tank proves his courage by fighting Veds, alien creatures which resemble the eponymous parasite in the horror movie *The Tingler* (1959) inasmuch as both feed "on fear" (Leeder 785) and can cause their victims to die of fright.

In place of a Tin Woodman, Sass has Kel-Paten (known as the "Tin Soldier"). The Tin Woodman, like Kel-Paten, was gradually rendered less and less human:

> the Wicked Witch enchanted my axe, and when I was chopping away at my best one day [...] the axe slipped all at once and cut off my left leg. [...] So I went to a tinsmith and had him make me a new leg out of tin. [...] When I began chopping again my axe slipped and cut off my right leg. Again I went to the tinner, and again he made me a leg out of tin. After this the enchanted axe cut off my arms, one after the other; but, nothing daunted, I had them replaced with tin ones. The Wicked Witch then made the axe slip and cut off my head [...]. But the tinner happened to come along, and he made me a new head out of tin [...] the Wicked Witch [...] made my axe slip again, so that it cut right through my body, splitting me into two halves. Once more the tinner came to my help and made me a body of tin, fastening my tin arms and legs and head to it, by means of joints, so that I could move around as well as ever. But, alas! I had no heart now, so that I lost all my love for the Munchkin girl, and did not care whether I married her or not. (Baum 29–30)

Despite his nickname, Kel-Paten is not actually made of tin but Dr Eden Fynn describes the process by which he was transformed from human to "biocybe" (Sinclair, *Games* 4) in terms which create parallels with the method by which the Tin Woodman lost his limbs:

> His dislike of medical facilities was well known. She didn't blame him. If someone had cut off her arms and legs when she was a teenager and replaced them with biocybernetic limbs,

she wouldn't have pleasant memories of the place either. (29)

Sass first meets her Scarecrow when he, like the original, is "not feeling well" (Baum 16) and it soon becomes apparent that although his head is not "stuffed with straw instead of with brains" (Baum 18–19) he is greatly troubled by "an implant in his brain" (Sinclair, *Games* 66). Sass's third companion is no cowardly Lion but as a telepath she is at particular risk of succumbing to Ved-induced "Fear [...] If you can link to it, it grabs something you remember, makes it worse, until you want to die" (339). The companions must triumph over a fearsome female enemy wearing "the austere purple and black robe of a Nasyry warrior priestess" (358) who is as evil as the Wicked Witch of the West and, before Sass can return home, she must escape from a place of illusion known as "McClellan's Void" (308) which could be thought of as a much more dangerous version of Oz's throne room.

Heeding Sinclair's request to "Ask" rather than behave like her professor, I emailed her to find out if she'd intended to create parallels with Baum's novel. She responded that:

> *The Wizard of Oz* has long been a favorite of mine—more so as the movie with the wonderful Judy Garland [...]. But it wasn't the inspiration behind GAMES. Kel-Paten's story—to me—has always been a cross between Pinocchio and Beauty and the Beast. ("Facts" 29 May)

She later added that:

> The whole Pinocchio thing for me is [...] the "wants to be a real boy" part. [...] Pinocchio [...] was a manufactured creation, as is Kel-Paten. [...]
>
> Kel-Paten also owes some to Styx's "Mr Roboto" [...] and to the Trek characters of Spock and Data. Did I think of all this FIRST before I wrote him? Hell, no. Did some of this occur to me while writing? Hell, probably. I did initially write Kel-Paten and Sass in the mid to late 1980s [...] just as characters in various vignettes and, as well, later (or about that time) as characters in a Star Trek fan-fic writing group I belonged to. [...]

Kel-Paten['s] [...] in love with the "creation" of Tasha Sebastian—just as he himself is a creation. Tasha is a fiction or
at least that's how she views it. So we have one person's idealized creation (the Kel with Kel-Paten) in love with another
fictional creation (the identity of Tasha hiding the reality of
Lady Sass). Again, did I set down one day and say, "Oh, now
I'm going to write a story based on Pinocchio and Beauty and
the Beast and include themes of self-perception?" Uh, no. I'm
not that smart. ;-) Did I see those kinds of things AFTER the
first draft or two? Uh, yeah. I tend to look for things like that.
("Facts" 30 May)

Sinclair's description of her creative process provides support for
Northrop Frye's rather startling claim that while "Criticism can talk,
[...] all the arts are dumb" (4): Sinclair's "first draft or two" made
"a *disinterested* use of words" (Frye 4) inasmuch as they did "not
address a reader directly" (Frye 4) in order to send her a message.
Indeed, unless an author intends to write either a satire or a didactic
work of fiction, it seems unlikely that she would sit "down one day
and say, 'Oh, now I'm going to write a story based on Pinocchio
and Beauty and the Beast and include themes of self-perception
[...]'". If she did, the result would probably lack vitality, its plot and
characterisation overwhelmed by the imperative to teach the reader
a lesson. According to romance author Jennifer Crusie, "the best
of what we do comes from the subconscious soup that's bubbling
away beneath our logic" and therefore, when writing that "first draft
or two", the author is "not required to put all the pieces together.
The girls ["our instincts, the Girls in the Basement"] say, 'You don't
need to know what [any particular aspect of the text is] about right
this minute, because you'll over-analyze and overwork it and ruin
everything.'".

Awareness of the "Girls in the Basement" means that "It is not
only tradition that impels a poet to invoke a Muse and protest that his
utterance is involuntary" (Frye 5). Laura Kinsale, another romance
author, asserts that:

The creative process is quite different from what many people seem to imagine. Contrary to appearances, there is someone, or something outside of the creator that is involved [...] it is the source of all artistic endeavor. Since the ancient Greeks, human creators have sacrificed and prayed in awe of the power of the Muse. [...]

My books are mine, and yet they are alien to me—as a child belongs to a parent and yet has a life of its own. I can guide and hope and nudge my characters this and that way, but in the end, they become what they become. ("Renegade")

Thus when, "AFTER the first draft or two" (Sinclair "Facts" 30 May), an author with "some critical ability of his own" (Frye 5), who is "able to talk about his own work" (5), sees its themes and becomes aware of hitherto opaque sources of inspiration, that author is acting as a literary critic of their own work.

For Frye the pronouncements of the author-as-critic therefore have "a peculiar interest, but not a peculiar authority" (5). He may well be correct that another critic, not the author of a work, will be "a better judge of the *value* of a poem than its creator" (5). The author's statements about his or her intentions and influences should not, however, be completely discounted. For example, an author's truthful account of how a work was revised in order to bring out the themes that he or she, in the guise of critic-of-her-own-work, had perceived in it, will offer valuable insights to a critic. That said, "generating a work with a particular meaning is [...] something one can fail at" (Irvin 116). Even if we accept that a talented author will not fail to make her meaning clear to "a careful, appropriately informed audience" (122), the involvement of a muse, or the subconscious, in the creation of the early drafts of a work makes it unlikely that the author-as-critic will be "aware of all the meaning potential of the work she has generated and of its relationships to other works, historical events, and so forth" (123). Indeed, it seems highly unlikely that *any* critic could be aware of all the potential meanings of a work, as well as of its direct and indirect relationships to other works and to its historical context. A contemporary critic, for example, may well catch allusions that would baffle or be missed by a critic working on the text after the passage of a couple of hundred years. That later critic, however, is likely to have the benefit of hindsight and a distance from the original context which permit the making of new assessments of the ways in which the text reflected on and responded to its historical context.

There are, then, limits to the authority of both critics and authors-as-critics and I hope, therefore, that despite Linnea Sinclair's disavowal of the suggestion that *The Wizard of Oz* was a source of inspiration for *Games of Command*, it will not seem wholly illegitimate to suggest that it may have had a subtle, subconscious influence. It is also possible that some of the similarities I perceived are due to Pinocchio and Data, Kel-Paten's acknowledged literary ancestors, sharing some cultural genes with the Tin Woodman: Doran Larson, for example, has suggested that one can trace the modern line of "wanna-be-human robots and cyborgs from Baum's Tin Man to *Star Trek*'s Data" (64). At the very least, I hope I will be absolved of attempting to force the novel to mean "what I choose it to mean—neither more nor less" as I turn my focus towards Sinclair's acknowledged sources.

In common with Kel-Paten, "the Triad's *biocybernetic* admiral" (Sinclair, *Games* 3), Pinocchio, the Beast, Data and Spock are not considered entirely human. In addition, in much the same way that the Beast hopes to return to his original state, Pinocchio wishes to become a "real boy" and Data's desire is "to be fully human (repeating the trope of the robot who wants to be a man that is immediately familiar at least from the time of the Tin Woodman of Oz)" (Joyrich 66), Kel-Paten desperately wants:

> to make Tasha see him as something—some*one*—other than a biocybe construct [...] to convince her that underneath the hard cybershell that was Admiral Kel-Paten, there was a man named Branden who was still very much human. Or part human. (Sinclair, *Games* 100)

Unlike Pinocchio, Data and Spock, however, Kel-Paten, like the Tin Woodman and the Beast, found himself in his less-than-fully human condition as the result of a transformation. The Beast at least remained a fully biological being but Kel-Paten did not. In this he therefore more closely resembles the Tin Woodman, who has been described as a "well-known cyborg" (Stefoff 10); "*Star Trek*'s Data, in contrast, is an android, a robot that is completely artificial but is made to look and act as human as possible" (Stefoff 10–12). Like Pinocchio, Data is not, and never has been, biologically human or part-human. Dennis Weiss links this lack of humanity to his lack of emotions:

> As we regularly watch [...] Data [...] attempt to understand what it is to be human, we are given an object lesson in why it is that [he/it] cannot be human. In these object lessons, *Star Trek* affirms the importance of human embodiment, feelings and emotions, love, spontaneity, the unconscious, family, and culture. (11)

Unlike Data, Kel-Paten is part-human, "disconcertingly so" to Sass, who had "expected someone—some*thing*—less *human* in that black uniform and trademark black gloves. And definitely not as male" (Sinclair, *Games* 8). In his masculinity, and in his control over his emotions, he would seem more closely to resemble Spock. If so, his relationship with Jace Serafino, like Spock's with Kirk, may be read as an exploration of contemporary masculinity and the ways in which 'real' men are expected to express their emotions.

Although in humans the "physical and mental capacity to have emotions is universal, [...] the ways those emotions are [...] elicited, felt, and expressed depend on cultural norms as well as individual proclivities" (Rosenwein 836–7). Those norms can be taught subtly, by example, or made explicit, as in the following passage from a fantasy romance by Mercedes Lackey in which the heroine recalls an occasion on which two children with the same emotional reaction were treated differently:

> she remembered two children who must have been the same age, sitting on the grass of the racecourse [...] crying after being thrown almost identically. One was a boy, and one a girl. The girl had been picked up by her nanny, petted, cooed at and taken off for cake. But the boy had been pulled up to his feet by his caretaker, his shoulder had been given a shake, and he had been told in no uncertain terms that he was shaming his father and he was to stop crying and be a man.
> And he had.

And she had known at that moment, with complete aston-
ishment, that the world was unfair. Sometimes it was worse to
be a boy. (359)

There can be significant variations in what it means to be a 'real'
man. In the US, for example, the:

> eighteenth-century model of manhood, identified by histori-
> ans as "republican" or "communal," set forth that a male, as
> head of household, place the good of the community above
> individual desires, that he subordinate self-interest to the com-
> monweal. In the early nineteenth century, this accepted gender
> construct came under assault from the market economy's pro-
> tagonist, the "liberal" or "self-made man," who unapologeti-
> cally pursued wealth, power, and self-advancement. (Laver 1)

In order to encourage this self-making:

> Middle-class parents taught their sons to build a strong, manly
> "character" as they would build a muscle, through repetitive
> exercises of control over impulse. The middle class saw this
> ability to control powerful masculine passions through strong
> character and a powerful will as a primary source of men's
> strength and authority over both women and the lower classes.
> [...] The mingled honor, high-mindedness, and strength stem-
> ming from this powerful self-mastery were encapsulated in
> the term "manliness." (Bederman 11–12)

This restrained, early-nineteenth-century ideal of masculinity was,
however, soon challenged by a:

> bodily ideal of manhood which had only begun to emerge
> in the first half of the nineteenth century, [but] became the
> dominant ideal in the second half. [...] A true man was now a
> physical creature, full of animal qualities and primitive urges.
> Men took nicknames like "Tornado" and "Savage" that con-
> nected them to basic natural forces. They feared that humans
> had "put reason in place of instinct, and are going to no good
> end." [...] The good man was not, however, a victim of his
> own physical impulses. He took pride in his powerful will

which vanquished laziness and lust. (Rotundo 26–7)

These relatively rapid changes in the way masculinity was constructed, and the co-existence of differing ideals of manliness, demonstrate that "Manhood—or 'masculinity,' as it is commonly termed today—is a continual, dynamic process" (Bederman 7).

It was certainly in flux in the mid-twentieth century when Gene Roddenberry created the early instalments of *Star Trek*: "All the marginalized groups whose suppression had been thought to be necessary for men to build secure identities began to rebel" (Kimmel 174) and "the 'masculine mystique'—that impossible synthesis of sober, responsible breadwinner, imperviously stoic master of his fate, and swashbuckling hero—was finally exposed as a fraud" (173). According to Michael S. Kimmel:

> *Star Trek* revealed, perhaps more clearly, if unintentionally, than any other TV show, the growing crisis of masculinity. Here manhood was divided into two halves—the rational, abstract, and emotionally invulnerable alien, embodied in Mr. Spock, and the aggressive, erotic, and intuitive traditional version of manhood, expressed by Captain Kirk. […] Neither was complete, and therefore neither could serve as a role model for the future. Full manhood could not even be reclaimed in space, the "final frontier". (191)

In *Games of Command* Kel-Paten and Serafino appear to resemble the masculine archetypes embodied by Spock and Kirk in the original *Star Trek* but, as Ferguson, Ashkenazi and Schultz argue happens in *Star Trek: The Next Generation*, Sinclair's text "often plays with conventional gender boundaries and practices in unconventional ways" (215).

Early in the novel Sass describes Kel-Paten as a "six-foot-three deadly emotionless son of a bitch. That was the whole point. No emotions to sway decision-making. Only cold, hard clinical facts" (Sinclair, *Games* 93–4). As such he, like Spock, would seem to exhibit:

> some of the qualities considered most admirable in men in patriarchal society: extreme rationalism accompanied by emotional repression, great physical power, and, most importantly,

the ability to dominate every situation. (Cranny-Francis 282)

Kel-Paten's obsession with Sass makes him demand her presence on his ship (and her consequent demotion from Captain of the *Regalia* to "new first officer on the *Vaxxar*" (Sinclair, *Games* 3)) so that "I know where you are, I know you're safe, I know I can protect you" (184). This, his higher rank, his extreme "physical strength three times that of a normal human male" (103) and enhanced mental abilities which "gave him analytical capabilities that matched—and at times exceeded—the computer systems of the best hunterships" (103) would seem to indicate that he is likely to be a rather typical "alpha male" romance hero. This type of hero is, however, "a figure who tends to be as sexually experienced as he is powerful, masterful, and—at least as the novel begins—emotionally reserved" (Allan) and it is eventually revealed that Kel-Paten, who has loved Sass unrequitedly for twelve years, is a virgin. Sass, by contrast, is experienced sexually but, like many an "alpha" hero, has always remained heart-whole: "Hot sex was such a great stress-reliever. But love ... she couldn't risk that" (Sinclair, *Games* 324). The role reversals continue as they consummate their relationship and, afterwards, Sass worries quite unnecessarily that "She'd been too aggressive; some men didn't like that. He needed to make the first move and she'd taken away that prerogative. She scared him off" (453).

The gender reversals in the protagonists' sexual histories and behaviour are revealed relatively late in the novel but it is quickly apparent to the reader that no romantic relationship in which Sass is involved is likely to reinforce the notion that "women being the gender in touch with caring emotions would give men love, and in return men, being in touch with power and aggression, would provide and protect" (hooks 101). Instead Kel-Paten, who has "the same emotions, fears, desires, and joys as any other human male" (Sinclair, *Games* 100), finds himself in a romantic relationship which in many ways embodies the feminist ideal as described by bell hooks:

> The heartbeat of our alternative vision is [...] there can be no love when there is domination. Feminist thinking and practice emphasize the value of mutual growth and self-actuali-

zation in partnerships [...]. This vision of relationships where everyone's needs are respected, where everyone has rights, where no one need fear subordination or abuse, runs counter to everything patriarchy upholds about the structure of relationships. (103)

Even before Sass knew how Kel-Paten felt about her, and well before she came "to the most amazing, incredible realization" (Sinclair, *Games* 392) that she loved him, she nonetheless considered him a friend, or at least, although unsure that he could experience friendly feelings,

> she realized that it mattered little what a 'cybe was capable of. The extension of friendship was equally her responsibility.
> If they weren't friends, they were at least colleagues. (146)

As such, she did not hesitate to show "intense disapproval" (139) of some of his actions, even though he had the capacity to "toss her across the room. Or sear her with a touch and she'd be dead before she hit the floor" (138). Clearly, Sass did not "fear subordination or abuse" (hooks 103); rather she "just ... trusted him" (Sinclair, *Games* 109) and later that trust extends to mutual revelations of feelings of inadequacy.

Kel-Paten's biggest fear is that, as a biocybe, perhaps "in spite of all the counterfilters and sub-routing he'd implemented—everything that had once made him human was finally programmed out of him" (104) and he may therefore not be "someone she could love—scars, synthderm, wrist ports, and all" (444). For her part, Sass believes that her true identity makes her unlovable: "*I'm* not the top-of-her-academy-class well-bred Tasha Sebastian you fell in love with. I'm not anyone you *could* fall in love with" (413). By sharing her fear she enables Kel-Paten to learn "that Sass's inner demons weren't all that different from his own" (Sinclair "The Admiral") and she herself comes to realise that they both have:

> scars [...] full of pain and bad memories. [...] Unpleasant. Best kept hidden.
> She understood that [...]. She had scars. But hers were inside, while his were on the outside. (Sinclair, *Games* 447–8)

The "scars" may be "Best kept hidden" from most other people but Kel-Paten and Sass do not continue hiding them from each other; in laying themselves open emotionally, understanding each other's fears, and loving each other, emotional and physical "scars [...] and all" (444), they display the kind of love described by bell hooks, a love "rooted in recognition and acceptance, that [...] combines acknowledgment, care, responsibility, commitment, and knowledge" (104).

As for their professional relationship, although Kel-Paten outranked Sass, he never dominated her. Rather, they "clashed, amicably, for years" (Sinclair, *Games* 44) and having worked together for six months "She really believed they'd developed a level of mutual respect" (151). She "enjoyed testing the depths of his cybernetically perfected mind" (16) and "he encouraged her input" (16), partly because "I work better if you're there to punch holes in every hypothesis I come up with" (39). At their very first meeting he was struck by her ability to scramble computer "codes with a flair that's more than impressive" (181) and as far as her job as Captain is concerned, he knows that "she can handle a Triad huntership without a hitch" (99).

Yvonne Tasker has argued that:

> images and narratives focused on military women disrupt very directly assumptions that behaviors or qualities designated masculine are reserved only for men. Obviously they are also framed by ongoing, hard-fought arguments concerning the proper role of women in the US military. (209)

It was not until 2012 that Jeannie Leavitt, the woman who "became the Air Force's first female fighter pilot in 1993" (Schafer), also "became the first female to lead an Air Force fighter wing" (Broadway). Leavitt's 1993 appointment came as:

> In the 1990s the combat taboo was gradually eroded, with women making some significant progress in Western militaries, especially the United States, Canada and the Scandinavian countries. (DeGroot 28)

It was only in January 2013, however, that "Defense Secretary

Leon E. Panetta [...] announced the end of the direct ground combat exclusion rule for female service members" (Roulo).

Ground combat is not a normal part of Sass's work as captain of a huntership but her decisive responses in McClellan's Void would seem to "disrupt very directly assumptions that behaviors or qualities designated masculine are reserved only for men" (Tasker 209): they challenge the commonly held belief that "Women [...] do not make good soldiers because they are weak, both physically and emotionally" (DeGroot 23). Here, without even needing to plan out her response to an enemy,

> she just grabbed his rifle with one hand, lunged forward, and planted a knee to his groin. She thrust the weapon up as he arched toward her. It slammed into his face. Blood spurted. (Sinclair, *Games* 396)

By the end of the scene, Sass has "taken down two of the best-trained mercs in the business" (397); she may be small and female, but she is certainly not physically weak. Nor, at critical moments in the text, does she allow her emotions to override her professionalism. Unlike *Star Trek: Voyager*, whose final episode "shows us the apparent end result of feminine leadership; a bitter old woman willing to compromise her ethics and her sense of self for purely emotional reasons" (Bowring 394), *Games of Command* offers the reader a female leader who is not prepared to "risk [...] the lives of every empath and telepath in the Alliance, just because her heart was breaking" (Sinclair, *Games* 509). Sinclair's positive depiction of "feminine leadership" also ensures that, unlike *Voyager*'s Kathryn Janeway, who is "punished for being a leader" (Bowring 402) by being condemned to the "lonely and sad life [...] of the prison in which her leadership keeps her" (Bowring 395), Sass retains the love of her telepathic pet furzel, enjoys a close friendship with her female chief medical officer, and is eventually reunited with Kel-Paten.

There is, perhaps, only one aspect of Sass and Kel-Paten's professional relationship which could arguably reinforce or reflect gender stereotypes about men and women's abilities:

> Kel-Paten [...] looked for the known, correlating and synthe-

> sizing, while she looked for the unexplainable. Granted, his cybernetically enhanced thought processes were a million times faster than hers, but he was linear, where her analysis tended to do pirouettes and somersaults. (Sinclair, *Games* 19)

This might seem to endorse the "equal, but different" (Chesser 21) view of the sexes in which it is accepted that:

> women are largely guided by an intuitive sense. Men generally tend to adopt a more 'rational' attitude. They usually pride themselves upon this. But it must be confessed that masculine decisions are not generally sounder than intuitive feminine ones. (35)

This statement comes from a 1950s guide to marriage rather than from a starship flight-training manual but might nonetheless be held to encapsulate the reason for the differences in Sass and Kel-Paten's styles of problem-solving—were it not for the presence in the novel of Jace Serafino, a male character whose approach to his work is, if anything, even more intuitive than Sass's. In his "creativity" (Sinclair, *Games* 43), or use of "Unorthodox methodology" (43–4), Jace is, as Kel-Paten observes, "not unlike [...] Tasha" (44).

Jace Serafino embodies, but also poses certain challenges to, the figure of the "aggressive, erotic, and intuitive traditional version of manhood" (Kimmel 191). He is:

> Male. Humanoid. Approximately forty-one years of age. Six foot three and one-half inches. Two hundred twenty-two pounds. [...] Right from the tips of his scuffed boots to the gray pants that hugged well-muscled thighs, to the torn shirt that revealed a flat, hard stomach, to the square jaw with that damnably attractive cleft, to his night-dark long hair that escaped its careless tie and now lay against his shoulders—he was unequivocally gorgeous. (30–1)

He is also "a charming rogue, always hip-deep in some kind of trouble" (15) whose "effect on women was legendary" (42). There would therefore appear to be clear parallels between his attitude towards women and that of Captain Kirk whose "traditional sailor behavior left him with a woman in every port" (Ferguson, Ashkenazi and Schultz 217):

> most of Kirk's relationships are the love 'em and leave 'em [...] variety. Kirk was always able to triumph over the relational distractions the women represented to his primary love affair with his ship. Kirk's promiscuity was most often merely physical; he actually fell in love only a few times. (217)

Unlike Kirk, however, Jace's masculine personality has been deliberately shaped by an external force known as Psy-Serv:

> a vicious, insidious, power-hungry agency that was far beyond the control of any rational governmental authority. Its proponents lauded it as the great protector, an eradicator of the unscrupulous. Sass doubted any Psy-Serv agent would know a scruple if it bit him in the ass. (Sinclair, *Games* 64)

Jace's telepathic abilities have been inhibited by "an implant in his brain, courtesy of Psy-Serv" (66) and his personality has therefore split into two: there is "a tremendous benevolence" (61) in the telepathic Jace but the other is "not my better part" (73). It is the non-telepathic Jace who is "a rake and a scoundrel, who has only one use for beautiful women—and it's not friendship" (74).

As for Kel-Paten, the processes which transformed him into a biocybe have altered him both physically and emotionally: "A properly functioning biocybe was not supposed to experience emotions" (55) or at least, not emotions like love, which "Psy-Serv would dismantle him for experiencing" (23). In order to deny him emotions, Psy-Serv installed "emo-inhibitor programs" (93); they seem, however, to have had little concern about him feeling "anger [...]. It was the only emotion that came easily to him, because Psy-Serv didn't bother with any serious inhibitors there. They wanted him angry and they wanted people afraid of his anger" (99). Nonetheless, as Sass comes to realise, Kel-Paten is not just a "Tin Soldier. He was Branden. He had bypassed all those emo-inhibitor programs and loved her" (343). The two most significant male characters in this novel, then, constantly attempt to circumvent the psychological restrictions imposed upon them and they do so because they are not naturally hard-wired to exhibit the Spock and Kirk types of masculinity.

They have, instead, literally been artificially hardwired in ways which are intended to inhibit particular emotions and abilities and the intended limitations in their emotional repertoires mirror those often ascribed to men who are only metaphorically hardwired:

> turn to the opening page of *The Essential Difference*, a highly influential twenty-first-century book about the psychology of men and women, and there you will find Cambridge University psychologist Simon Baron-Cohen expressing much the same idea: 'The female brain is predominantly hard-wired for empathy. The male brain is predominantly hard-wired for understanding and building systems.' (Fine xix)

Cordelia Fine suggests that what is often ascribed to "hardwiring on closer inspection starts to look more like the sensitive tuning of the self to the expectations lurking in the social context" (13). Lurking behind the social context on board Kel-Paten's starship is Psy-Serv, which can take extreme measures to enforce the norms it has established with regards to telepaths and biocybes. Dr Eden Fynn, the chief medical officer on the *Vaxxar*, is not a member of Psy-Serv but because she has accepted its norms regarding biocybes, when she begins to suspect that Kel-Paten is deviating from "the rational, abstract, and emotionally invulnerable" (Kimmel 191) ideal of manhood, she fears she may have "to file a Section 46 on him" (Sinclair, *Games* 52), alerting the authorities to "behavior, attitude, and/or reactions clearly in contradiction to the accepted norm" (94). The way in which Kel-Paten's emotions are monitored and diagnosed creates a parallel with the way in which, in contemporary societies,

> Negative and hostile feelings can be shaped and transformed by doctors and psychiatrists into symptoms of new diseases [...]. In this way such negative social sentiments as female rage and schoolchildren's boredom or school phobias [...] can be recast as individual pathologies and "symptoms" rather than as socially significant "signs." [...] In this process the role of doctors, social workers, psychiatrists, and criminologists as agents of social consensus is pivotal. (Scheper-Hughes and Lock 27)

Kel-Paten himself, however, resists attempts to pathologise him and is more than prepared to critique the system:

> Overriding my emo-inhibitors was something I'd been doing for quite some time. First of all, it was a tremendously flawed program. Anger is permissible but affection is not? Emotions aren't that cleanly divisible. Once I realized how easy it was to be angry, it wasn't that difficult to test to see if other emotions could break through. (Sinclair "The Admiral")

The device Psy-Serv had implanted in Jace's brain has led him, too, to an important realisation. By exaggerating the division between the two sides of Jace's personality, the implant inadvertently alerted him to what might, were he a biocybe, be called flaws in his basic program. As he tells Dr Fynn telepathically:

> I'm a rotten son of a bitch out there. [...] I was pretty much the same son of a bitch before the implant. What the implant did is force me to look at myself. And it's allowed me to become, with you, someone I might have been if my life was different. (Sinclair, *Games* 164)

I would not go so far as to suggest that, in a novel which she described in the dedication as a "bit of space opera romance silliness", Sinclair consciously set out to write a critique of contemporary gender norms and the ways in which they are socially enforced. It is, nonetheless, what I believe she achieved and she herself has acknowledged being drawn to science fiction romance because "You can toss all known societal edicts and cultural mores out the window, or viewport (as the case may be). Characters don't have to fit defined roles (as we know them)" (Lawson).

One might, therefore, wish to explore the possibility that the villains of *Games of Command*, the Ved, share a number of traits with patriarchy. On a superficial level, one can observe that each Ved takes the form of "A glowing blue orb" (Sinclair, *Games* 360) and blue is a colour currently associated with masculinity. On a more profound level, the Ved is "like a parasite, feeding on hatred. Fear" (339) and, as one would expect in a parasite, it requires a host:

> The human—the host—eventually died. But until that point, the Ved provided the human with a feeling of invincibility, power, omnipotence—whatever the human craved. And the human *would* crave, because the Ved needed more emotions to feed on. (450)

In *Games of Command* the host experiencing the feelings of invincibility states that the events which are unfolding as a result of the Ved's intervention are "A game of ultimate control" (362). Allan G. Johnson's analysis of patriarchy suggests that it, too, manipulates its (mostly male, but occasionally female) hosts via fear and the promise of control:

> Perhaps more than anything else, what drives patriarchy as a system [...] is a dynamic relationship between control and fear. Patriarchy encourages men to seek security, status, and other rewards through control, to fear other men's ability to control and harm them, and to identify being in control as both their best defense against loss and humiliation and the surest route to what they need and desire. (53)

Perhaps Sass's idea about how to deal with the Ved-created Void also has some applicability to patriarchy: "don't give Bad Thing anything to work with. No more secrets, no more lies. No more games" (Sinclair, *Games* 412).

Intriguing though the parallels are, one would have to be a tenured member of Professor Dumpty's Department of Creative Etymology to insist that the true meaning of "Ved" is "patriarchy". In the game of command between author and critic, I do, however, feel it possible to state that this "bit of space opera romance silliness" portrays the relationships between emotions and gender in a way which is complex and thought-provoking, not least because it foregrounds ways in which an individual's personality, identity and self-perception can be shaped by their socio-political context. The following chapter takes a closer look at how, by demonstrating a quality which is highly valued in his socio-political context, an individual can change the identity ascribed to him.

Workers

This "Workers (W21-1) symbol sign […] may be used to alert road users of workers in or near the roadway" (593)..

2. *Simple Jess*'s Work Ethic

Writing from Lancaster, Pennsylvania, in July of 1835 Michel Chevalier, a Frenchman, declared that in the United States:

> The habits of life are those of an exclusively working people. From the moment he gets up, the American is at his work, and he is engaged in it till the hour of sleep. Pleasure is never permitted to interrupt his business. (283)

It is a description representative of the accounts offered by European observers who "were amazed at the intensity with which Americans approached work and business" (Bernstein 159). Admittedly visitors such as Chevalier may primarily have been:

> describing not ordinary laborers but their own social counterparts, particularly merchants of moderate means [...]. Work was the gospel of the bourgeoisie, above all of the Protestant bourgeoisie, but it was not for that reason simply a subcultural peculiarity. In the American North, as nowhere else in the Western European orbit, the middle classes set the tone and standards for society as a whole. (Rodgers 15)

Working-class "mid-19th century British and Irish immigrants to the U.S." were also "amazed at the speed and regularity of native workers" (Stott 88) and later in the century the Knights of Labor, who at their peak in 1886 included perhaps "as many as 20 percent of all workers" (R. Weir 16, n. 32), declared in their initiation ceremony that:

> In the beginning God ordained that man should labor, not as a curse, but as a blessing; not as a punishment, but as a means of development, physically, mentally, morally, and has set thereunto his seal of approval, in the rich increase and reward. (Commons and Andrews 22)

Albeit in modified form, a belief in the improving power of work continues to unite US society. In 2004, for example, Barack Obama made a speech to the Democratic National Convention in which he argued:

> that all Americans shared common values that transcended politics. Obama clearly viewed his personal story as a microcosm of a larger story, the American Dream. He was one of a multitude of Americans who had risen from humble beginnings, with hard work and perseverance. (Rowland and Jones 435)

The success achieved by Jesse Best, the eponymous hero of Pamela Morsi's *Simple Jess* (1996), is much less spectacular than Obama's but his work ethic is no less exemplary:

> He did his share and more. And he did it with such a light heart as if work itself was not a burden, but a privilege. *Maybe*, she thought, *he knows better than the rest of us.* (223)

The story of Jesse's work is inseparable from that of his love, as in the nineteenth century, when:

> Striving to the fullest in the economic realm [...] was identified by men [...] with loving a woman. They turned to economic accomplishments not only as proof that they were doing their social duty, but also as a sign of their emotional commitment to a woman. For some men romantic love claimed a more powerful pull upon their economic performance than any abstract concern for usefulness, scarcity, or moral decay. By the early nineteenth century, the work ethic for middle-class men may also have been an ethic of love. (Lystra 136)

Since the setting for Jesse's and Althea's courtship and married life is also the place where they work, *Simple Jess* supports Charles H. Hinnant's theory that "the distinction between the economic sphere and the sentimental sphere, so familiar to us in the modern world, is precisely what the genre of romance seeks to contest" (164). The "ranching activities" in many romances set in Montana, for example, "don't speak primarily of sound business practice and land management; they speak of husbandry, of sensuality, of 'Nature' as procreative force" (Cook 66); the same may be said of the farming tasks in Morsi's novel, set in rural Arkansas in 1906.

The very first task Althea sets Jesse makes her aware that "His voice was deep and sharp with authority. It had a warm, masculine timber. Althea found herself genuinely enjoying the sound of it" (Morsi, *Simple* 31). Later, as he milks the cow, she observes that "His every movement was made with exceptional grace" (38) and as:

> Jesse worked, vigorous and eager, upon the boards of the platform he had built [...] his [...] thin cotton shirt was now plastered to his muscles like second skin. His pale blond hair was damp with perspiration and glowed golden in the eastern sunshine at his back. He was strong and virile and excitingly male [...], he was beautiful. (255)

Work's influence on the "sentimental sphere" is not limited to showcasing Jesse's physical attractions: it also helps him give expression to his feelings. Jesse's respect for Althea's wishes is evident at the communal hog killing when he declares that "This first one is Miss Althea's hog [...] So we'll do whatever she wants done" (244), and when he goes hunting, it is because he "wanted to put meat on her table. That's what men do for the women they love" (103). Conversely, when he expresses admiration for the results of Althea's labour, she senses that she herself is valued. He praises her cooking, which is a skill Althea:

> had worked hard to learn and it was good to be appreciated. [....] It was good to hear the words aloud. It made her feel ... it made her feel somehow like cooking was really worth the trouble. (42–3)

Love, even when in the incipient stages, seems to imbue work with meaning and so, not long after Jesse's "first day as the hired man" (48):

> the workdays seemed to go faster than expected for Althea.
> It was strange, the mere fact that there was another person at the place made day-to-day progress and accomplishments seem bigger and better. (52)

Love definitely increases Jesse's productivity: "as each day passed, Jesse worked harder and longer and faster for Miss Althea" (98). With his work expressing his love and care for her, and his appreciation of her work hinting at the extent to which he respects and values her, the sentimental and economic spheres overlap such that work becomes a labour of love. That Althea fully appreciates this is demonstrated by her response to Jesse's promise to "Work for you 'til my back is broke and my fingers is down to the bone. And love and care for you until the day I die" (312): she thinks his is "the most beautiful marriage proposal I've ever heard in my life" (312).

A Hero's Work

The ability to work hard is "a valued male characteristic adopted by the writers of romance" (Cohn 43). Admittedly, at times it may be difficult to separate the value ascribed to hard work from the appeal of its most dazzling fruits. This would seem particularly true of novels in which the work that propelled the hero from poverty to a position of wealth and power is only described briefly or in retrospect. It is often the case that:

> despite the emphasis on occupation, we do not see the heroes at work. What is shown is […] the evidence of successful work: possessions, cars and houses and clothes, yachts and servants, rich gifts and exotic vacations. (Cohn 46)

In addition, when a hero's success is due to exceptional talents or personality traits, it might be argued that it is these, and not merely his capacity to work hard, which are valued. In Jayne Ann Krentz's *Trust Me* (1995), for example, it was Sam Stark's "prowling, predatory intelligence" (15) as well as his capacity for hard work which enabled him to found a company that:

> advised many of the largest Northwest businesses […]. Word had it that Stark, who had started with nothing three years ago, was now, at the age of thirty-four, as wealthy as many of his clients. (11)

By contrast Jesse Best is a man who "works hard. In some ways harder than other men, because things in this world don't come easy to" him (Morsi, *Simple* 261–2) and who is often depicted working hard. He is also a hero who feels he would have fulfilled his every ambition if only he could acquire "his own gun, his own dogs, and … and, well, he wanted a woman" (101). While he has had some experience with other people's guns and dogs, a woman seems literally out of his reach since:

> he had never touched a woman. He had never spilled his seed inside one.
>
> Pa had said that he couldn't, not ever. Pa said that no daddy on the mountain would ever want Jesse for a son-in-law and that it was best if he just not think about such things. (108)

The reason Jesse is such an unlikely candidate for a son-in-law and, indeed, a romance hero, is that he has an intellectual disability and "while physical disabilities continue to proliferate in popular romance, only a very few novels take on cognitively disabled main characters" (Baldys 128). Against the odds, however, and after much hard work and perseverance, Jesse gains a pack of dogs, a gun, and the love of a good woman.

That his success is a direct consequence of hard work seems particularly significant in view of Rosemarie Garland Thomson's observation that:

> Nowhere is the disabled figure more troubling to American ideology and history than in relation to the concept of work: the system of production and distribution of economic resources in which the abstract principles of self-government, self-determination, autonomy, and progress are manifest most completely. (46)

The inhabitants of Marrying Stone, Arkansas, are certainly troubled when Jesse's sister reminds many of them that "A bad fall or a bump on the head or a spell of apoplexy can injure the mind of anyone, anyday" (Morsi, *Simple* 261): "The truth of her statement was sobering to all" (261). Disabling accidents and illnesses raise questions about the extent to which any individual can be self-governing and self-determining. More concretely, a newly acquired disability often has a negative impact on an individual's work. In the US in the nineteenth and early twentieth centuries, for example:

> disabling injury or illness forced workers to take unskilled positions that offered lower wages. A vacuum cleaner salesman who earned $60 a week in the early 1920s before losing his right arm above the elbow in a work accident, for instance, could afterwards only find work as a telegraph messenger at $60 per month. (Rose 8)

Disability may thus pose a "threat to Americans' belief in the link between 'hard work' and economic and social success" (Garland Thomson 48).

Jesse, however, although he initially appears to lack "self-government, self-determination, autonomy" due to his disability, begins to show signs of all three when he sets about "buying me some dogs" (Morsi, *Simple* 21) from Althea Winsloe, and Morsi's novel ultimately validates "American ideology". In contrast to "dependent cripples [who have] symbolized the antithesis of American citizenship, challenging America's identity as the land of opportunity" (Byrom 135), Jesse is a character whose story endorses the:

> values [...] at the heart of the American Dream [which] are both personal (hard work, responsibility, determination, and so forth) and societal (freedom, potential for upward mobility, inclusiveness, community cohesion, and empowerment). (Rowland and Jones 431)

Having learned from his "permanently lamed" (Morsi, *Simple* 119) father to "do the best that ye can with what ye got" (120), he seizes the opportunity to realize his "three secret ambitions" (101) and thanks to both hard work and support from a variety of individuals within his community, he succeeds.

Working Towards a New Identity

Work has a particularly important role to play in changing Jesse Best's identity because he has an intellectual disability and "the disabled social category is harder to escape and far more stigmatizing than youth or age, which are seen more as stages in the lives of productive people than as immutable identities" (Garland Thomson 51). Attitudes towards those in "the disabled social category" have varied, however, and in some periods and places, it may be easier to escape the category than in others. For instance:

> In 1835, Thomas Cameron was a young postmaster in rural North Carolina; ten-year-old Lloyd Fuller was studying alongside his older brothers in their middle-class New England home. Thomas and Lloyd would today be considered developmentally disabled; in the 1830s, that difference alone did not disqualify them from work, education, social invitations, or travel. (P. Richards 65)

By contrast, in "the first third of the twentieth century, the 'menace of the moron' loomed as a perceived threat to the American way of life" (Keely 207).

As the new century began, "the eugenics era was gaining momentum, and social reformers sought segregation and prohibitions on marriage and procreation by people with disabilities" (Braddock and Parish 39). *Simple Jess* is set in 1906 and some characters in the novel do express concerns about "marriage and procreation by people with disabilities". Early in the novel Beulah Winsloe (a member of the McNees clan) insists that she would not want her widowed daughter-in-law Althea to marry into the Piggott family (of which the Bests form a branch). She claims that "the Piggotts [...] brung feeblemindedness to the mountain" (Morsi, *Simple* 5) and she goes on to state that "Simple Jess is feebleminded and Pastor Jay's senile. That's the kind a minds ye can get with the Piggott clan" (142). Although Jesse's relatives argue that "Being simple is not something that was carried to Jesse in the blood, it was a thing that happened to him when he was born" (261) because he "came into the world with the cord wrapped 'round yer neck" (119), Jesse and Jay's impairments are undeniable and are "true embarrassments for the Piggott family. The belief that such weaknesses were carried 'in the blood' was not a superstition easily overcome" (142). Given Beulah's general opinion of the Piggott bloodlines, it is unsurprising that she should be fiercely opposed to a union between Althea and Jesse: "as the girl's family we can't let it happen. […] He's simple. All their younguns could be simple as well!" (318).

Nonetheless, despite the concerns expressed about Jesse's disability and the attempts made to block his marriage to Althea, there is never any suggestion that his community sees a need for the segregation which, elsewhere in the country, was being achieved through institutionalisation: "In 1900, the census of mental retardation institutions in the United States was 11,800 persons" (Braddock and Parish 37). In the remote Ozark community of Marrying Stone, however, conditions would appear to be more akin to those in the post-revolutionary period, when "Physically able simpletons found no great obstacle to day-to-day living" (Trent 7). In such a setting Jesse may be stigmatised as "Feebleminded, simple, slow-witted, unsound" (Morsi, *Simple* 120) but he is also afforded the chance to change his status in the community.

To do so his identity must break free of one stereotype of disability without slipping into another: neither the seemingly benevolent stereotype "that people with disabilities are saintlike, cheerful, asexual, childlike, and unusually heroic" nor its mirror-image, which portrays them as "inherently unable to manage their own lives, embittered and malevolent, and morally, intellectually, and spiritually inferior" (Creamer 26), would allow him to be seen as a competent adult male.

Initially, Jesse does seem to fit the "saintlike, cheerful, asexual, childlike" stereotype. As the novel opens, there is something infantile, or perhaps girlish, about the way he "giggled out loud" (Morsi, *Simple* 10). Although he wears a "cap of homespun gray" (9) rather than a red riding hood, and is distracted not by flowers but by mushrooms "at the side of the path" (9), he resembles the young protagonist of a certain well-known fairy tale in having been sent on an errand, instructed not to "dawdle" (9), and warned "to keep your guard up when they's strangers about" (13). Certainly he would seem to have more in common with an innocent child than with either a huntsman or a big bad wolf. Looking at him, Althea sees eyes full of "innocent warmth" (58) and notes that his "expression was totally free of perfidy or guile" (24). Furthermore, in accordance with the "particularly ingrained image [...] of God as divine Father and human (especially a disabled human) as child" (Creamer 50), Jesse is declared to be "a favorite of Heaven. [...] The Good Lord did command to 'come unto me like a little child.' Our Jesse sure always does that" (Morsi, *Simple* 157).

Jesse's childhood was extended by his disability: as he says himself, "there ain't no feller on the mountain that felt like a boy longer than I did" (125). Indeed, in certain respects he is still considered a child by others because it is believed that "The feebleminded were only oversized children; little boys in the bodies of men, that's what folks said" (53). When Jesse, in his eagerness to earn Althea's dogs goes "running at first light" (29) to her house, rousing her half-dressed from her bed, she comforts herself with the thought that:

> he was simple. He probably thought no more of seeing her than if she were his sister. [...] It wasn't like she'd invited a *man* into her house when she was half-naked. Jesse Best wasn't a man, not exactly. He was big, like a man, and looked like a man, but ... well, he was something else entirely. (30)

That "something else" is "a child in a man's body" (306).

Deborah Marks has observed that, "Given the cultural expectation that people with learning difficulties are like 'innocent' children, it can be particularly difficult to recognise sexual knowledge" (47). An example of this type of failure can be found in one of the early interactions between Jesse and Althea. Jesse has "seen hogs bred and hounds mating" (Morsi, *Simple* 108), he knows that for a woman to have had a baby, a man must have "covered her" (37) and that, "if the noise from Roe and Meggie's bed was any clue, they did it pretty regular" (37). However, when Jesse mentions that in the early hours of the morning his sister Meggie had still been "lollin' in the bed with her man" (30), Althea, who immediately blushes and thinks of "*making babies*", assumes that "Simple Jess wouldn't know anything about that. Surely, he only meant that his sister still slept" (30).

Misconceptions about the sexual knowledge possessed by people with intellectual disabilities have often had practical consequences for their sex lives:

> Historically service models have been predicated on the need
> to maintain sexual boundaries between people with learning
> disabilities and the general public. 'Innocence' models sug-
> gest the need to protect people with learning disabilities from
> predatory members of the public, while 'degenerate' models
> stressed the need to protect the public from people with learn-
> ing disabilities. (Brown 125)

Althea would seem to continue to subscribe to the "innocence" model
even after Jesse has kissed her, and therefore feels that acting on her
attraction to Jesse is immoral:

> There was nothing legal or moral about kissing Jesse Best. It
> had been sin, plain as day. Breathless, heart-stopping sin. And
> one of the worst kind. The sin of taking advantage of a lesser
> creature. (Morsi, *Simple* 161)

Jesse's opinion of his arousal in response to seeing Althea in her
underclothes suggests that, rather than being "lesser" than Althea,
he is in fact quite similar to her. Although he knew she must have
engaged in sexual activity with her husband, he thought she:

> probably didn't know nothing about how a man felt. But she
> smelled so good, and he'd seen her round parts real clear, and
> he just couldn't help but get hard about it. […] It wasn't right
> for him to be getting hard about Miss Althea. (34)

Thus although neither Althea nor Jesse know it, it is clear to the reader
that the attraction is a mutual one and that both would be capable of
giving meaningful, informed consent to a sexual relationship with
the other.

Their community, however, initially takes a very different view.
When Jesse reveals that he has "kissed Althea Winsloe" (183), "the
crowd went into disbelieving shock" (183):

> For folks on the mountain, simple and sex didn't go together.
> That was a thing to be feared. His faintest gesture of kindness
> to the young girls would be suspect. And that way he had of

standing quietly among the ladies as if just enjoying being near them would now make the womenfolk uneasy. (185)

To them, the revelation that Jesse is capable of sexual desire raises fears that he is a disabled person of the "embittered and malevolent" sort from whom the public need to be protected. Such fears are groundless, however, since Jesse knows that:

> There was lots of rights and wrongs when it came to mating and people. Jesse didn't know all of the rights and wrongs. But he did know some of them. (33)

Jesse not only knows the rules; he also acts on them. When he first came to work for Althea, for example, he accidentally saw her in her underclothes and "got hard" (33) but, since he "knew that it was wrong for a man to see a woman in her josie [an undergarment] if she wasn't his sister or his wife [....] He'd kept himself facing the hearth 'til it eased off" (33).

Morsi's depiction of Jesse thus challenges both the "innocence" and the "degenerate" models of intellectual disability: he is neither angel nor devil but rather "every bit as human and as fraught with human frailties as the rest of us" (262). Nonetheless, Emily Baldys warns that:

> we must be critical not only of depictions that seem obviously overdetermined and fantastical, but also of those that seem realistic or believable; and [...] we must attend to the ways in which even seemingly inclusive, well-intentioned texts [...] *create* versions of disability that crowd out alternative or transgressive ways of being. (139)

It is true that the depictions of all three of the disabled characters in Morsi's novel are uniformly positive. However, whereas Baldys argues that the novel is "invested in the fantasy that disability can be 'overcome' through heteronormative romance" (135), I would suggest that in *Simple Jess* any "narrative rehabilitation" (128) of characters with disabilities is achieved primarily through a focus on their work ethic.

Jesse is "huge, dependable, and work-brittle [industrious]" (Morsi,

Simple 26) and his "strength, willingness, [...] biddability" (254–5) and capacity to "concentrate [...] fully on what for others might well have been a boring, repetitive task" (207) mean that he has much to offer an employer. Although he cannot always "force the right words [...] into his brain" (73) and "order up the terms and phrases in the order needed" (72), he does not need them to perform manual labour. In fact, in the long term his disability may even make him a better worker because although it impeded his ability to learn the skills he required:

> Once mastered [...] he never forgot them and he rarely allowed his concentration upon them to slip. [...] Jesse worked steady and sure, long after others had tired, and he always seemed quite happy to do so. (223)

Jesse was taught how to farm and hunt by his father, "bright-eyed and jovial" (144) Onery Best, who also has a disability and long ago decided that although he is lame he "cain't just sit around [...] and say, 'Ain't it a shame I'm a cripple.' [...] I walk where I got to go, plow when they's no help for it" (120). Pastor Jay, though he has "lost his mind" (11) and officially retired, still watches over his flock and is on hand to offer theological and spiritual insights. Even Sawtooth the hunting-dog is still "a good tracker" (34) despite the confrontation with a bear which had "smashed his mouth up pretty good and broken most of his teeth out" (34).

Jesse and the dog have more than disability and a work ethic in common:

> The mind of the dog was in many ways as simple and uncomplicated as Jesse's [...]. He was taught to memorize actions in places he couldn't reason, and obey in situations that he did not understand. (100)

As a result, both Jesse and the dogs are treated as inferiors: "Most men, knowing themselves to be a lot smarter than [...] dogs, often overruled their judgment" (100) and since "Everyone understood that" the "feebleminded could not think" (53) they treat Jesse in much the same way. Thus although Jesse wants "to be like other men" and the narrative acknowledges that "In many ways, he was" (8), he is "underestimated" (255) to the point where he is not really considered a "man", and certainly not one with the ability to support a family. That this is so was made very clear the:

> last time Jesse had worked for Mr. Phillips, unloading a mule train carrying hundred-pound sacks of flour from the mill, [and] the storekeeper had paid him only five pieces of licorice.
>
> Of course, his brother-in-law had come back down the mountain with him the next day and insisted that Jesse get paid a man's wage.
>
> But the storekeeper had hoped to get a day's work from him for five pieces of candy. [...] Men don't get paid with candy. (17)

In much the same way that Jesse and his labour were undervalued by Mr. Phillips so, in the "mental retardation institutions" of the time:

> Residents worked laundries, farms, and workshops, not so much to develop skills for community out-placement but rather to contribute to the self-sustaining economy of the institution. (Braddock and Parish 37)

These individuals worked, then, but there was little likelihood that their work would change their dependent status because it was not believed possible to "make out of the *real idiot* a reasoning and self-guiding man" (Samuel Gridley Howe qtd. in Trent, 30).

Initially Jesse does appear to lack the capacity to be "reasoning and self-guiding". In the opening chapters of the novel he is shown on his way to Mr. Phillips's store, having been "given the responsibility of going for supplies" (Morsi, *Simple* 8). This is "a job that a man would do" (8) and Jesse "wanted to [...] tell Mr. Phillips what he was there to buy. That's what other men did" (8). Unfortunately, Jesse is distracted by the news that Althea is selling her dogs and it is only thanks to the intervention of Mr. Phillips and the existence of a shopping-list written by his sister that he is able to complete his task. It therefore seems that, to quote Samuel Gridley Howe, a nineteenth-century expert on the treatment of "idiots", Jesse "must ever [have] a child-like dependence upon others for guidance and support" (qtd. in Trent, 30).

While it is true that Jesse does require support in some areas, it could well be argued that everyone does to some extent. The other men at the hog killing, for example, "depended upon him to do the heavy work" (Morsi, *Simple* 254). As for his ability to be "reasoning and self-guiding", it had not been fully tested until he offered to buy Althea's dogs. This was due to the fact that he had primarily worked under the supervision of his father, Onery Best. Although Onery is "loving and accepting" (50) and "allowed his son as much freedom as Jesse chose to take" (50), there were, nonetheless, "times when he questioned his son's ability" (50) and "worried that Jesse would make a mistake, a mistake that might hurt him and somebody else" (50). His first conversation with Jesse about what needs to be done on Althea's farm, and in particular about which type of tree would provide the best fuel is thus, as Jesse recognises, "a test" (50) of Jesse's ability to both identify and solve problems independently. Slowly and thoughtfully, Jesse answers the questions and at last:

> Onery Best gave his son a big approving smile. "Eat up, boy," he said. "A man what earns his own living needs to get plenty of vittles in him." (51)

Jesse has proven to Onery that he is truly capable of working not with a "child-like dependence upon others for guidance and support" but like any other "reasoning and self-guiding" man.

Althea has rather less foreknowledge of Jesse's capabilities and so she begins from the premise that:

> she couldn't expect Jesse to know what had to be done and when to do it. He was simple. It was her task to tell him what to do and see that he did it. [...] He had a strong back and a willingness to work. Those things, however, would be wasted if he didn't receive the proper guidance and direction. (54)

When she tries to stop him "wasting his time cleaning up the field" (54) this is, in effect, a second test and one to which Jesse responds by outlining his plans for tree-cutting, hog-killing, and hunting before bringing Althea to a state of "near disbelief" (58) by pointing out that the contents of the field will provide food for the cow during the winter.

Although being "a great provider" (142) is an important part of a husband's work, Jesse must also prove that he can provide a child with paternal care if he is to be deemed marriage material. He does so when, despite his disability, he is the only adult to realise "It's wrong" (235) for Althea's young son, Baby-Paisley, to wear a deer tail on his "hat like Dan'l Boone" (233). Jesse is, however, unable to articulate the reason for his unease so Althea tells him that he's "just confused on this one" (238). Subsequent events prove that he was, in fact, wholly correct. When out hunting with Althea's two suitors Jesse sees:

> the white flash of a deer's tail. [...] He looked back at Eben and Oather, both taking aim.
>   He knew then. Suddenly, clearly, he knew. [...] Throwing himself in the firing line, Jesse pushed the rifles aside. (289)

His instincts and quick intervention have saved the child's life and taken together the three tests prove that Jesse is correct when he claims in his marriage proposal that he "can be a good husband to you [...]. I can get you game. I can keep up this farm. And I care about your boy" (312). On the day he brings "Baby-Paisley home from that hunting trip" (312) Althea decides he is "the man that I want to marry" (312).

It is a decision supported by Granny Piggott, who is "the matriarch of the mountain" (129) and "the expert on family" (317), vigorously defended by Pastor Jay who, despite his senility, is still able to refute the new pastor's statement that the marriage went "against the Bible" (317), and endorsed by Althea's father who, after the new pastor claims "A woman has to do what her daddy tells her" (321), rubber-stamps his daughter's decision. While the transition from widow to wife will bring Althea economic and emotional security, the changes it brings to Jesse's status are even more far-reaching because this is his first marriage, and in their community it is marriage, and not physical maturity alone, which confers full adult status on an individual: "Marriage was an important sacrament on the mountain. It was a rite of passage to adulthood" (131). The endorsement of the union by three representatives of matriarchal, ecclesiastical and patriarchal power can therefore be considered this small community's equivalent to the granting of full American citizenship, which Judith N. Shklar has described as membership:

> of two interlocking public orders, one egalitarian, the other entirely unequal. To be a recognized and active citizen at all he must be an equal member of the polity, [...] but he must also be independent, which has all along meant that he must be an "earner," a free remunerated worker, one who is rewarded for the actual work he has done. (63–4)

Judged solely on the egalitarian basis of age, Jesse was theoretically entitled to be considered an adult and thus "an equal member of the polity" but in practice his disability had hitherto relegated him to dependent status and denied him recognition as a fully adult inhabitant of Marrying Stone. By working for Althea in a considered and autonomous manner, however, Jesse demonstrated his entitlement to the status of a "free remunerated worker", and the ensuing public acceptance of his right to become a husband and father indicates that he has at last been recognised as a full citizen of his community; his story indicates the importance of the work ethic in American culture.

Afterword

Morsi dedicated *Simple Jess* to her daughter, Leila, "One of God's favorites", whom she has described elsewhere as having "an intellectual handicap with decreased cognitive functioning and multiple developmental delays" ("Sarah"). Jesse, too, is "God's favorite" (*Simple* 157), but Morsi was well aware that this would not necessarily or automatically make him a favourite with romance readers. She has written that:

> As a "Special Needs Mom" my world has always been filled with lots of differently-abled people and those kinds of char- acters routinely make it into my stories. [...] My publisher was understandably leery. Jesse is no typical romantic hero. He is special in so many different meanings of that word. Would readers accept him?

> To be completely honest, buyers didn't rush in for this story. Sales lagged, readers were hesitant, but slowly, slowly a few people read it. They told other people, who told other people, who told other people. No book I have ever written has generated so much positive feedback. ("SIMPLE")

It seems probable that readers would have been even more hesitant had Jesse been unable to demonstrate that he "wasn't a boy, he was a man" (70). He is fortunate that the hard work his community values is primarily manual labour. In another place, at another period in time, or in another social class, the opportunity afforded Jesse to change his status through hard work might not have been available. For example, elsewhere Morsi has written about an individual with an intellectual disability whom she knew personally and:

> who truly loved cleaning. He loved the broom, the mop, the dust rag. He was thrilled with the power to change the whole look of a white porcelain sink with only a damp sponge. It was such a feeling of accomplishment. His father, a successful, high powered executive was incensed that his protected, privileged child, despite his handicap, would choose such menial work. Although there was clearly a place of employment for his son's skills, the father insisted that he would never allow his child to pursue work as a janitorial helper. This was obviously not about the son, but the preconceptions and values of the father. ("Sarah")

A Prairie Schooner

This style of covered wagon became a symbol of westward expansion.

3. Go West, Young Woman

Americans have prided themselves on living in "the land of the free", a land of opportunity where individuals can shape their own identities and destinies; nowhere in the US is more closely identified with this freedom and opportunity than the West, for:

> the epic America of the frontier, America as a mythical West, had been turned into a symbol of freedom long before the consumption revolution. The West as a beckoning yonder [...] kept alive the dream, in far-away corners of Europe, of a life lived in freedom and independence. (Kroes 468)

Given its almost mythical status and the way in which its borders shifted, it seems fitting that even today, "in almost every book or article written about the frontier or the West" (Thompson 68), there:

> is [...] a vagueness about the West's location. Where is it? Is Dallas in the West? Hawaii? What about those older places that were once the West like Illinois or Louisiana? [...] If the West as a region is unfocused and vague, the definition of *frontier* is equally imprecise. When and where does the process commence and terminate? (Thompson 69)

I too shall remain vague about the physical location of the West because I will be focusing on the West's "mythological meaning in modern American culture" (Spurgeon 6), with the term "myth" defined here as "a story that contains a set of implicit instructions from a society to its members, telling them what is valuable and how to conduct themselves if they are to preserve the things they value" (Kittredge 62). Given this focus on the myth, and the fact that New Western Historians argue that:

> The story of the region's sometimes contested, sometimes co-

operative relations among its diverse cast of characters and the story of human efforts to "master" nature in the region, are both ongoing stories, with their continuity unnecessarily ruptured by attempts to divide the "old West" from the "new West". (Limerick 63)

I shall not separate romances with contemporary settings from those with historical ones. Any such attempt would, in any case, be complicated by the fact that two of the romances analysed here explicitly link events in the present to those in the past.

In addition, having prioritised the study of the "mythological" nature of the West, it seems permissible to become almost as unconcerned about genre boundaries as about geographical and chronological ones. After all, questions similar to those raised by Thompson might also be asked about genre definitions: genres change and expand over time, and it seems impossible to create fixed boundaries between them. The Western, the genre most closely associated with the American West, and the popular romance novel, may appear to be the antithesis of each other. The romance is a form of fiction which has been described as "a literature written almost exclusively by women for women" (Williamson 126) while the Western is often considered to be a form of fiction "in which men prove their courage to themselves and to the world by facing their own annihilation" (Tompkins 31) and which came into existence when:

> Appalled by the coy complacencies of late-nineteenth-century 'little women', turn-of-the-century writers such as Owen Wister and Zane Gray [sic] offered the male reader something supposedly closer to his own experiences. [...] The action takes place against a harsh backdrop of deserts and windswept plains, constructed as an unsuitable locale for the niceties of womanly feeling. (Stoneley 224)

Nonetheless, the West has in fact proved to be an eminently suitable locale for romantic love and in romance fiction "the ranching and cowboy West seem to have enduring popularity" (Cook 56).

That romance novels should have conquered the West is perhaps not so surprising when one considers firstly that "much of the literary West's recurring preoccupation is with marriage, the unexpected but inescapable lens through which writers [...] focus on the West's ongoing national significance" (Handley 2) and secondly that "genres are <u>not</u> mutually exclusive: [...] any two (or ten) genres can combine within the same work in parallel, in series, or in fusion" (Lennard and Luckhurst 51). Indeed, Westerns may include romantic plots or subplots which are brought to a happy conclusion. Examples include Owen Wister's *The Virginian* (1902) which "became the paradigm text of the Western film genre" (Slotkin 169), *The Light of Western Stars* (1914) by Zane Grey, who "popularized the form in the wake of Wister's prototype" (McVeigh 47–8), and *The Burning Hills* (1956) by Louis L'Amour, "Grey's successor as the poet laureate of Westerns" (Cawelti 2).

The Burning Hills depicts a hero who subscribes to the theory that "there were in a man's life certain ultimate things and just one ultimate woman" (L'Amour 54) and, because "words did not come easily to him and yet he knew, desperately, that he must finds words to reach this woman", he struggles to "make her realize that he loved her, that he really wanted her" (103). As the novel closes, however, it would appear that he has at last succeeded.

Romance also flows through Wister's *The Virginian* although, in accordance with its hero's belief that "good women were to know only a fragment of men's lives" (Wister 295), the novel restricts romantic love to a "fragment of" the text. Nonetheless, if romantic love is frequently present "either not at all, or, as an undercurrent, deep out of sight" (174), whenever its hero has concluded "Whatever he was a-doin' in the world of men" (230) he returns to his sweetheart and, after "she has kept him waiting three years" (242), they marry, produce "many children" (327) and are forecast to "live a long while" (327) together.

A later incarnation of this novel is invoked in the opening pages of *The Light of Western Stars*: Gene Stewart's appearance in the "dingy little Western railroad-station" (Grey 3) of El Cajon, New Mexico "recalled vividly [...] that of Dustin Farnum in the first act of 'The Virginian'" (6). Unlike the Virginian, however, Gene is "pretty drunk" (11) and has "made a fool bet I'd marry the first girl who came to town" (12). He therefore proceeds to force the newly arrived Madeline Hammond, "one of the most beautiful, the most sought after, the most exclusive women in New York City" (21), to marry him. Matrimony would appear to be almost contagious in this novel: it was because there had been "a *fiesta*—and a wedding" (12) that Gene made his drunken bet. Moreover, he and Madeline are the first of four couples to tie the knot during the course of the narrative although Madeline, the reader, and even for much of the novel Gene himself, remain unaware of the validity of the ceremony which was hastily conducted in the station's waiting-room by a terrified Spanish-speaking priest. Madeline buys a ranch and employs Gene as her foreman; he strives to become worthy of her but since she remains "dead to love, to nobility that she had herself created" (353) he leaves for war-torn Mexico "to invite the bullet which would give her freedom" (352). This impels the priest to tell Madeline the truth; the shock of learning of her marriage and impending widowhood awakens her to "consciousness of her own love" (349). She speeds south to save her beloved from a firing squad and the novel ends with her standing before him, acknowledging herself to be "Your wife!" (389).

Women in the West

The heroines of both Wister and Grey's novels are Easterners and to this day many Western romances begin "with a young woman's decision to leave the sedate and orderly American East [...] in order to venture to a more turbulent and risky region, namely the American West" (Bettinotti 172). Although Westerns and the West have been strongly associated with men and masculinity, L'Amour's hero states that "A man can't make it alone. Needs him a woman. These here city women, they look mighty nice but a man out here needs a woman who can walk beside him, not behind him" (105). The hero of one Western romance has similar requirements of a woman: she must be able to "carry her half of the burden. Ranching's a hard life. I can't afford to marry a woman who can't contribute her share to making things work" (Johnston 96).

The West would seem to require "a particularly western female type" (Baym 64) who can, when necessary, take not "a woman's part, but a man's part" (Wister 223) and she can be found in the Western "memoirs, novels, short story collections, histories, biographies, reportage, descriptive sketches, textbooks, poetry volumes, works for young people, political and social polemics, travel books, and more" (Baym 63) written by women between 1833 and 1928. This

> woman protagonist stands for what the West allowed women to become, what all women might become: hardy, capable, physically active, and—because she doesn't have to resort to female tricks and wiles—honest and forthright. This female type had emerged in American writing soon after the Revolution as a sign of women's access to freedom and opportunity. In its western version, the type made the West itself into the truest expression of the thoroughly American spirit. (Baym 64)

The gently-bred Eastern female protagonists of Wister's *The Virginian* and Grey's *The Light of Western Stars* are women who, willingly or not, are shaped by the West so that they come to embody this "thoroughly American spirit". Their literary descendants can be found in the pages of romance novels, including Joan Johnston's contemporary-set *A Wolf in Sheep's Clothing* (1991) in which the heroine, Harry, goes to Montana "to start over, to confront her problems and deal with them" (65) and "to prove that she could do anything she set her mind to do *on her own*" (75). In Mary Burton's historical romance, *A Bride for McCain* (2000), the challenge of Western living is faced unwillingly, as is evident from the following piece of dialogue between the hero and heroine:

> "I don't want to be a frontier woman. I like myself just the way I am."
> "Colorado's hard country. Nobody leaves it untouched." (36)

By the end of the novel, however, this heroine too has passed the test and, because she has been touched by both Colorado and her hero, she will not be leaving.

These two romances, along with Joan Wolf's *Affair of the Heart*

(1984), set in modern Wyoming, can be read as expressions of the American "Myth of the Frontier [...] our oldest and most characteristic myth" (Slotkin 10), which came into existence because:

> In America, all the political, social, and economic transforma-
> tions attendant on modernization began with outward move-
> ment, physical separation from the originating "metropolis."
> [...]
>
> Euro-American history begins with the self-selection and
> abstraction of particular European communities from their
> metropolitan culture, and their transplantation to a wilderness
> on the other side of the ocean where conditions were generally
> more primitive than those at home. [...] Thus the processes of
> American development in the colonies were linked from the
> beginning to a historical narrative in which repeated cycles
> of *separation* and *regression* were necessary preludes to an
> improvement in life and fortune. (Slotkin 10–11)

This is a narrative which can be found in the majority of novels discussed in this chapter: they feature a protagonist who has travelled to the West from an "originating 'metropolis'".

Separation from "the metropolitan regime of authoritarian politics and class privilege"

Nancy Cook has observed that romance novels:

> maintain and promote the West as a mythic and fantasy space,
> a pastoral world where intricate social constructs identified
> with urban culture have been sloughed away, revealing both
> an essential West and an essential character. (56–7)

This "essential character" is that of "The compleat 'American' of the Myth" (Slotkin 11) who, although he is no longer required to have "defeated and freed himself from [...] the 'savage' of the western wilderness" (11), continues to have "freed himself from [...] the metropolitan regime of authoritarian politics and class privilege" (11).

In Wolf's *Affair of the Heart* an opportunity to denounce Eastern politicians is provided by the revelation that Caroline, the heroine, works in Washington for a senator "who wants to put missiles over the entire West" (30):

> "Er," said Caroline gingerly, "not the *whole* West, Joe."
> The big rancher snorted. "Let me tell you what I think of those fancy Eastern senators," he said vigorously, and [...] proceeded to unburden himself of a [...] variety of deeply felt convictions about the sacredness of the land and the unholiness of the earth's despoilers. (31)

No counter-arguments are provided in support of Senator Williamson's plans for although Caroline attempts to qualify Joe's initial statement slightly, she has, nonetheless, "at one time or another thought all the things Joe was now saying" (31).

Caroline is closely associated not just with the Eastern political establishment but also with the social class which Jay, her hero, refers to as "the East Coast aristocracy" (29). She has received an "Eastern establishment upbringing", wears "designer clothes" and takes "holidays in the south of France" (135). Jay, like Mary Burton's Western hero in *A Bride for McCain*, is particularly wary of women with "class privilege" because bitter experience has taught him that such women are unsuitable mates for a Westerner, so before he meets Caroline his father warns her that:

> you're not going to find him—overly friendly. [...] He never forgave his mother for leaving [...]. No, you're not his mother, but you come from her world. You're from the East, like Nancy, and you're from the same kind of social background. (15)

Unlike Nancy, however, Caroline "would love [...] a life close to nature, to earth and grass and animals, a life where people had roots in the land" (70). Her suitability for such a life is demonstrated by her "grim fortitude" (90) in the face of injury and her ability to overcome pain through "sheer will" (90). These prove that she is "every bit as tough a nut" (20) as Jay and although she rides in the Eastern style, using a saddle which is "a tiny postage stamp of leather" (18) compared to "the huge western saddles" (17–18), her horsemanship "sure put the boys in their places but good" (129).

In Burton's novel it is Ross McCain's first wife, rather than his mother, who gave him a bad opinion of Eastern women. The pair:

> separated shortly after we married. Caroline returned to Chicago [...] She hated it here [...] Prosperity was a hard, lawless town then and no place for a lady. (73)

Jessica Tierney, who will soon become Ross's second wife, seems to resemble his first inasmuch as her clothing instantly marks her out as yet another incomplete American. In much the same way that "the villain's costume, especially that worn by the 'hired gun,' or professional killer" (Skerry and Berstler 81), makes him easy to identify in many Western movies, her:

> fancy dress [...], like her grace and poise, spoke of money, privilege and society. Firsthand experience had taught him that society types like her were trouble—big trouble. People like her had their own way of thinking and living, and were best avoided altogether. (Burton 84)

Jessica herself is initially unhappy about going West: on hearing that she will be heading towards Cheyenne, Wyoming, "The thought of traveling to such wild, untamed country made her cringe" (21). Having "been trained to be a society wife" (47) at "Miss Madeline's Academy for Young Ladies" (8), "one of the most respected schools for young ladies in the East" (164), she has, as Ross suspects, been prepared for a very different "way of [...] living". Her privileged education has taught her "proper etiquette" (165) but none of the "basic" (95) skills, such as "chopping wood, building fires in a potbellied stove or cooking" (95), which are required for life in the West.

Nonetheless, as the inhabitants of Prosperity, Colorado soon discover, Jessica has the strength of character to survive outside "one of those fancy, big-city drawing rooms" (30). The beginning of the process of separation from Eastern privilege is symbolised by the destruction of the "fancy dress": it is "ruined when she [...] discarded it by the pond" (127) so that she could swim to the rescue of "little Abe, [and] every man realized she had grit and spunk to go with her looks" (124).

"'Regression' to a more primitive and natural condition of life"

In accordance with the Myth of the Frontier, the heroines of these novels "experience a 'regression' to a more primitive and natural condition of life so that the false values of the 'metropolis' can be purged and a new, purified social contract enacted" (Slotkin 14). There is, however, considerable variation in the extent of the "regression" and the thoroughness with which the values of the "metropolis" are condemned.

A "'regression' to a more primitive and natural condition of life" is readily apparent in Johnston's *A Wolf in Sheep's Clothing* when Harry moves from Williamsburg, Virginia, to a "tiny Montana sheep ranch" (7). There are "cavernous ruts in the dirt road" leading to its "tiny, weather-beaten log cabin" (8). Inside, in the kitchen, the "walls and floor of the room consisted of unfinished wooden planks. A step down from 'rustic,' [...] More like 'primitive'" (17). It is equally clear that, by the end of the novel, Harry has established "a new, purified social contract" between herself and her family. When she informs her parents that she intends marrying Nathan and remaining in Montana, they accept her decision and welcome him into the family. This leaves her:

> stunned at her parents' acquiescence. [...] Had she only needed to speak up for what she wanted all these years to live her life as she'd wanted and not as they'd planned? Maybe it was that simple. But until she'd come to Montana, until she had met and fallen in love with Nathan, Harry hadn't cared enough about anything to fight for it. (184)

However, while conditions in the East enabled her to remain untrue to herself, the novel leaves it open to question whether the "values of the 'metropolis'" were actually false.

There is considerably less ambiguity about the morality of city life in Joan Wolf's novel but also rather less "regression" involved in moving to the "Double Diamond ranch house" (*Affair* 55). Since it is "really lovely" (55) and kept in immaculate condition by a housekeeper, it would presumably only seem "primitive" to someone like Nancy, who "was made for bright lights and lots of people" and couldn't "take the loneliness of the ranch" (100). While there is no explicit condemnation of Nancy, the "purified social contract" which will be enacted as a consequence of Caroline's marriage to a Westerner is clearly socially conservative and the effect of minimising the disadvantages of country life is to make Nancy's reasons for preferring the metropolis seem either frivolous or immoral.

Although Caroline's own morals are "certainly not orthodox" (86), she does "not believe in sex without commitment" (86) and her admission that she has received a "decadent Virginia upbringing" (50) is made "teasingly" (50) rather than sincerely. She is, in fact, a traditionalist who responds angrily to the suggestion that one of her ex-fiancés might have "suffer[ed] from Oscar Wilde's problem" (37): "'Oh!' Her cheeks flamed with color. 'No, he did not! Don't be disgusting'" (37). Her swift response clearly implies that it is homosexuality which is "disgusting". Furthermore:

> Although she would never have dared admit it to any of her liberated friends, Caroline had no hankering after a career. She wanted a man—*the* man—and marriage and a family. It might be considered a disgraceful ambition for a woman in this day and age, but still, there it was. It was all she had ever wanted. (69)

It is evident that Caroline, who "would look great on the cover of a magazine" (19), could also serve as a poster-girl for heteronormativity. She will achieve her ambition with the help of a man who makes his first appearance in the novel "tired and dirty and bloody from a day of branding and castrating and dehorning and inoculating cattle" (17). It could be argued that these activities are neither truly "primitive" nor "natural" but it is indisputable that they take place in Wyoming, a state described as having "some of the most spectacular and extensive areas of unspoiled land in the country" (49). It is a place where "The winters are hard" (173) but, as Caroline observes, "At least snow is clean [...] All you get in Washington or New York is slush and filth and dreariness. And in the summer you steam" (174). The symbolism is readily apparent: the moral code in Wyoming is as "hard" as its winters, but it is infinitely preferable to the filthy, steamy "false values of the 'metropolis'".

An "improvement in life and fortune"

At various stages in American history the type of progress or improvement to be achieved as a result of living on the frontier has been:

> defined in different ways: the Puritan colonists emphasized the achievement of spiritual regeneration through frontier adventure [...] while Jacksonian Americans saw the conquest of the Frontier as a means to the regeneration of personal fortunes and/or of patriotic vigor and virtue. (Slotkin 11–12)

Ross McCain, the hero of Burton's *A Bride for McCain*, acquired his "personal fortune" in the West. He:

> had been a captain in the Confederate army, then, after the war, had moved west. He'd hit upon a silver strike and had parlayed his find into one of the largest mining operations in Colorado. (Burton 27)

His fortunes continued to improve thanks to "Long hours in the mines and shrewd investments in cattle and railroads [which] had made him a very wealthy man" (183–4).

Romance heroines, however, are much less likely to achieve success through "shrewd investments". As Jan Cohn has observed, it is generally the case that "Romance fiction offers a fantasy of female success, specifically economic success, the aggressive nature of which it thoroughly masks under the heroine's extreme economic innocence" (127). Even in the West, then, a heroine's "improvement in life and fortune" will tend to be defined primarily in terms of love and the gaining of a committed romantic partner. Jessica Tierney, for instance, has "always wanted someone to love—dreamed of it—but in her heart, she'd never really thought it would happen" (Burton 226). The "improvement in life and fortune" she most desires is thus emotional rather than financial;

she finds it in the aptly named Prosperity, Colorado.

Regeneration through Violence

In the Myth of the Frontier "Violence is central" (Slotkin 11) to the reformation of society:

> the Myth represented the redemption of American spirit or fortune as something to be achieved by playing through a scenario of separation, temporary regression to a more primitive or "natural" state, and *regeneration through violence*. (Slotkin 12)

Joan Johnston quickly runs through the entire scenario in a paragraph replete with allusions to key events in US history:

> Like a pioneer of old, Harry wanted to go west to build a new life. She was prepared for hard work, for frigid winter mornings and searing summer days. She welcomed the opportunity to build her fortune with the sweat of her brow and the labor of her back. [...] This venture was the Boston Tea Party and the Alamo and Custer's Last Stand all rolled into one. In the short run she might lose a few battles, but she was determined to win the war. (35)

Here are all the elements of the Myth of the Frontier: the Boston Tea Party stands for separation from "the metropolitan regime of authoritarian politics and class privilege", the invocation of the figure of the "pioneer of old" suggests a "regression to a more primitive [...] state", the Alamo and Custer's Last Stand recall the violent struggle of White Americans against Native Americans and Mexicans, and all of these form the "necessary preludes to an improvement in life and fortune". Harry may only be fighting in a metaphorical sense but it is a metaphor which is sustained over the course of the novel: she has "come to Montana knowing there were battles to be fought and won" (173) and she works so hard, and for so long, that she experiences something "very much like battle fatigue. But then, wasn't she engaged in the greatest battle of her life?" (48).

Regeneration through violence is expressed physically rather than metaphorically, albeit in a somewhat vestigial form, in Wolf's *Affair of the Heart* when Jay, who is "the best shot in the county" (68) sets off into "the mountains" (105) with a posse to track down a "Mountain lion up by Montana" (67) which has "killed a whole lot of cattle" (67). After several days, and with their supplies beginning to run short, two of the men return. A few days later still, "Jim [...] came back. His horse went lame. Said Jay was going on by himself" (99). Alone in the wilderness Jay is in "very real danger" (105) as his separation from the ranch and "regression to a more primitive [...] state" is succeeded by "regeneration through violence". His success leads to his acclamation in Montana as "a national hero" (102) because with the earlier losses having cost "over five hundred dollars a head" (97) of cattle, the death of the lion eliminates a serious threat to the ranchers' economic viability.

"A new, purified social contract"

Jay's approach to predators would, however, almost certainly be condemned by Abigail Dayton, a "Fish and Wildlife agent" (Johnston 65) who appears in Johnston's novel and teaches the tenderfoot heroine that "You can't *shoot* a timber wolf! They're an endangered species. They're protected!" (69). Her attempt to convince Harry that "wolves weren't really as bad as people thought, and [...] their reputation had been exaggerated by all those fairy tales featuring a Big Bad Wolf" (68) can be seen as a counterpart, albeit small and inserted in a work of fiction, to the work of New Western Historians such as Donald Worster who, over recent decades, have scrutinised the types of "improvement in life and fortune" achieved in the West through violence and the creation of a "new, purified social contract". They took:

> a frank, hard look at the violent imperialistic process by which the West was wrested from its original owners and the violence by which it had been secured against the continuing claims of minorities, women, and the forces of nature. (Worster 16)

Worster thought that, having taken this "hard look" at the history of the West, Americans were "beginning to get a history that is beyond myth, [...] beyond a primitive emotional need for heroes and heroines" (16).

Romance fiction, however, has not gone beyond a "need for heroes and heroines" and romance authors have therefore adopted different approaches to reconciling this need with both the new Western history and the "Myth of the Frontier". Given that "the 'other' side in American history has been most typically Native Americans, and later Mexicans" (Spurgeon 150) and that this has often been the case in fiction too, one possible response to "the continuing claims of minorities" may be to desist from casting them as antagonists. Unaccompanied by any compensatory literary affirmative action, however, this may, as in Wolf's novel, lead to the creation of a fictional West in which there appear to be no non-White characters at all. Burton takes a somewhat different approach: she addresses racial inequality by having a secondary character briefly state that "I judge a man by the quality of his work, not by his past or the color of his skin" (90). Nonetheless, her Native Americans are no more than a picturesque part of the Western scenery, glimpsed as her heroine takes a first look at the West:

> she stood on the platform [...] staring at endless miles of desert and gray sagebrush dotted with a few weathered frame houses and shanties. A party of Indians wearing paint and armed with rifles watched the train as five rough-looking cattlemen drove their long-horned steers past a covered wagon pulled by six oxen. (24)

In any individual novel set in a state in which the vast majority of the population are White and in which there is only a small cast of characters, it may be realistic for there to be few or no non-White characters. Viewed collectively, however, a large body of such novels would seem to continue, albeit in a fictional and possibly well-meaning form, the "process by which the West was wrested from its original owners".

Another possible problem which can affect the representations of minorities has been highlighted by recent research which suggests that:

complementary stereotypical representations—those that depict relatively low-status groups as having their own set of
compensating rewards and high-status groups as having certain drawbacks—contribute to the perceived legitimacy of the
social system [...]. These representations communicate that
"no one group has it all" and thus encourage the feeling that
things somehow balance out in a way that makes the system
seem fair, or at least not unbearably *un*fair. (Kay *et al.* 313)

A representation of this kind can be found in Johnston's novel, in
which the White hero's housekeeper is an "old Blackfoot Indian
woman who [...] had mysteriously arrived [...] on the day Nathan's
mother had died" (40) and who has "clung to the old Blackfoot
ways" (41). Given that Katoya's narrative function is to offer Nathan
advice and she is described as having "eyes that were a deep black
well of wisdom" (41), she would appear to be a female version of
the "wise elder" stereotype: "wise elders are usually isolated from
other American Indians. They are mysterious loners whose role [...]
is to advise the White heroes" (Bird 71). Although this stereotype
places the "wise elder" in the service of the White hero, Katoya's
subordinate status is seemingly compensated for by the fact that she
possesses a deep wisdom to which he lacks access.

Complementary stereotypes may appeal to authors writing novels
in which a happy ending is guaranteed because, by helping to create
"a comforting illusion of equality", they bring the characters closer
to "living 'in the best of all possible worlds'" (Kay *et al.* 313).
Nonetheless, Pamela Regis has argued that at the beginning of every
romance the "world" in which the protagonists find themselves is
always "in some way flawed" (*A Natural* 31) and in a great many it
remains so, albeit to a lesser degree. This is certainly the case in two
romances which critique elements of the myth of the frontier: Ruth
Jean Dale's *Legend!* (1993) and Ruth Wind's *Meant to be Married*
(1998). Dale's novel is set mostly in 1876 but the actions in the
epilogue take place in "Showdown, Texas—today" (281) and thus
enable the author to show the persistence of a fabricated Western
legend: the novel's title is eventually revealed to be deeply tinged
with irony. Wind's contemporary romance covers a much shorter

span of time but her heroine's archival research into her family's history ensures that this novel also serves as an exploration of the ways in which Western history was falsified in order to create or validate myths. These romances thus complement the work of New Western Historians, who "have been creating a new history, clear-eyed, demythologized, and critical" for "this region that was once so lost in dreams and idealization" (Worster 7).

The new history has focused on people and issues that had previously been marginalised or overlooked. In addition, new perspectives have been brought to bear on those which are already well known. Dale takes this latter approach: she uses character types and situations which will be familiar to viewers of Westerns such as *Stagecoach* (1939), *The Gunfighter* (1950) and *The Man Who Shot Liberty Valance* (1962). As the novel closes, a newspaper is preparing to reprint a legend rather than the facts which would expose the hypocrisy and prejudice that underlaid life in the small town of Jones, Texas, when it was populated by a cast of characters which included an alcoholic yet competent doctor, a prostitute with a heart of gold, a gunfighter who knew he was "a marked man, [...] the target of every would-be gunman who crosses my trail. I've tried to outrun my reputation, but it's always right behind me" (Dale 179), and "a man of law, a peaceful man" (37) who was wrongly credited with shooting dead an evildoer who terrorised the townsfolk. What will become the "famous Texas legend of the gunfighter and the lady" (281) is concocted in order to give Boone, the gunman and hero of the romance, a means to escape his reputation; the storytellers "get away with it" (280) because in 1876 people chose to "believe what they want[ed] to believe" (280). The pretence is maintained in the present-day epilogue when a descendant of one of the original storytellers decides that the "writer-photographer team" which "a San Antonio newspaper" (281) has sent to interview him "didn't want the *real* story, they wanted the legend, just like everyone else" (282). One may find some justification for this belief in the fact that a real columnist for the *Arizona Republic* once responded to the New Western History by asking:

> Why can't the revisionists simply leave our myths alone? [...]
> Westerners—and most other Americans, for that matter—are
> quite content with our storied past, even if it tends to fib a bit.
> (Sunkel qtd. in Limerick, 63)

For the readers of *Legend!*, however, who have spent almost all of
the novel discovering the "*real* story" of the "gunfighter and the
lady", it is the "fib" which seems both revisionist and unsatisfactory.
We understand why it came into being, but we know it to be untrue.

Legend! is a narrative which demythologises the legends
concerning Boone the gunfighter and, by implication, calls into
question other myths and legends about the West. Thus although
there is "regeneration through violence" for the town of Jones,
which is reborn as Showdown, the novel as a whole suggests that
while violence may sometimes be an unavoidable response to a
dangerous situation, it often prompts yet more violence. In Jones,
for instance, when:

> the horse thieves became very bold [...] the men got together
> and decided to form the Vigilance Committee [...] then they
> caught one of the thieves red-handed [...] and hung him to the
> nearest cottonwood. (Dale 37)

This did indeed serve as an effective "deterrent to crime" (38) but
only until the horse thief's brother arrived with a couple of armed
henchmen "to get us a sheriff and a town" (244). Boone killed them
but had his success not been suppressed by the false legend which
cast him as the villain whose "outlaw gang" (282) threatened Jones,
it would have added to the reputation which set him apart from
others as surely as, but much less securely than, the mark of Cain.

Boone first became a "legend" when he was working as an assistant
marshal. One

> chilly January night [...] Booker Wall, a notorious Texas bad-
> man, indulged in his favorite pastime: using women as punch-
> ing bags.
>
> By the time Boone arrived on the scene, no room remained
> for compromise or reason. The situation called for gun jus-
> tice, pure and simple. The showdown, a classic confrontation

> on Main Street, was quick and clean—and for Booker Wall,
> deadly.
>   Later that same night, Wall's unsavory friends ambushed
> Boone, who shot two of them dead on the spot. A running
> battle with three others ensued; Boone shot two and the third
> bolted [...].
>   Boone didn't follow; he'd caught a bullet himself. Once up
> and around again, he found himself elevated to the status of a
> legend. (25)

Boone is clearly stated to have had no other option but to resort
to violence and it was exercised in an official capacity, in defence
first of the weak and then of himself; "Boone's actions, everyone
agreed, had been entirely appropriate to his position and the
occasion" (26). Nonetheless, the immediate reward he received was
not "regeneration" but rejection. Still worse, as a direct result of
the reputation gained in this incident, "Other men challenged him;
more lead was thrown" (26). Seemingly trapped in a downward
spiral of violence Boone knows that all he can look forward to is:

> constant danger and the possibility, even probability, of sud-
> den death at the end of the most innocent-appearing trail. A
> real home, children—these were not in the cards for a man
> with his reputation. (200)

He is, he says, "a man to be pitied, not held up as an example"
(219). There is, then, no glorification of violence to be found here,
nor is it presented as a morally regenerative force. Nonetheless,
since *Legend!* is a romance and he is the hero, Boone is eventually
regenerated through violence. Acting in self-defence he shoots
dead the "Colorado desperado" (241) who is the last of the men
threatening Jones. Since "A bullet had smashed into the man's face,
obliterating his features. It could have been any big, black-haired
man" (278), there is enough of a resemblance between Boone and
the corpse that the latter can be used as the basis of a legend in which
"the brave marshal outdrew the gunfighter Boone and shot him
down like a yellow dog on Main Street" (282). Having undergone a
"ritual death" (Regis, *A Natural* 35), the real Boone can finally "run

away from my reputation" (218); he and the heroine, Rose, move to California, where he makes "a fortune" (284).

There is a similar ambivalence implicit in the fact that the lies lead to "an improvement in life and fortune" for Jones: although "Instant fame as the final resting place of a renowned desperado brought rewards to the town in the form of growth" (283), none of the characters depicted in the novel seem to gain materially from this growth. Indeed, one of the two "pillars of the community" (12–13) who hoped that a showdown would help the town "get the county seat and that railroad line sure, and our troubles will be over" (142) "hadn't anticipated [...] that increased population would mean increased competition. In 1888, he gave up, declared bankruptcy and moved back east, a broken man" (283).

Jack Guthrie, the marshal, also departs, shaking "the dust of Jones, Texas, off my boots forever [...]. So much for the romance of the West" (278). Though he is "a better man for his adventures in wild and woolly Texas" (283), it is back East that he achieves "an improvement in life and fortune": having returned home he soon marries "a young woman he'd much admired before his departure" (283), has some children with her and, eventually, becomes "famous in legal circles by successfully arguing the controversial case of *Belsnapper vs. the State of Pennsylvania* before the Supreme Court" (284).

In direct contrast to the Myth of the Frontier, then, the narrative of *Legend!*, including the false legend which concludes with Rose and Jack, moving "to Philadelphia, where he took up the practice of law again. They never came back to Texas" (282), presents the reader with a scenario in which various characters flee from, rather than to, the frontier. Furthermore, there is no attempt here to depict the West as a place where all of "the false values of the 'metropolis'" have been "purged and a new, purified social contract enacted". In Jones, as elsewhere in the US, "the tenets of respectable society" (Dale 200) "separate women into good and bad categories" (8) and ensure that women have "a hard row to hoe. So many things were forbidden to them, and those who trespassed paid the penalty of public disgrace" (200). Libby Bowman, for example, is deemed "no lady, she's a whore" (70). When Rose attempts to defend her, Sally Curtis is outraged and declares that "my papa is right—you'd take up with a heathen Chinaman!" (104). The lines demarcating "respectable society" thus clearly exclude non-Whites as well as fallen women. Since neither Libby nor Tonio Ryan, who is "used to racial slurs" (55) because his "pa was Irish and [...] ma half-Mex and half-Injun" (95), will find "an improvement in life and fortune" on this part of the frontier, they too join the exodus from Jones: "Tonio [...] left town [...] in the company of the prostitute, Libby Bowman" (284).

Some may prefer the "fib" of the Myth to the more complex realities of the West's past and present. In Dale's novel, for instance, Thom T. Taggart reconciles himself to "tellin' all those lies about his Great-Aunt Rose and Great-Uncle Boone" (282) with the thought that:

> All that could be gained by the truth at this late date was eco-
> nomic ruin for the city of Showdown, Texas, which relied
> upon the annual celebration of Showdown Days for financial
> stability. (282)

There may, however, be negative consequences to clinging to the Myth of the Frontier. Patricia Nelson Limerick, another New Western Historian, argues that:

> We cannot take ourselves and our present challenges seriously
> [...] until we take our history seriously. We cannot live respon-
> sibly in the American West until we have made a responsible
> and thorough assessment of our common past. (64)

This is a task undertaken by Sarah Greenwood, the heroine of Ruth Wind's *Meant to be Married*; she eventually realises that she cannot continue to live in her hometown in the American West unless those closest to her both accept the truths uncovered in the course of her "responsible and thorough assessment" of their "common past" and act on them.

Sarah begins her research in the reference section of a library in Taos, New Mexico, where she informs the librarian that "My family has been at war with the Santiago family for more than a century

[...] and I decided I was tired of the legends and want to get the facts" (Wind 211). As in Dale's novel, it is the legend rather than the facts which are to be found in the local newspaper. In September 1859 it reported:

> the story Sarah had heard over and over again, all of her life. From her grandparents and her father, and on the lips of sympathizers. Emily Greenwood had been brutally set upon and raped by Manuel Santiago. [...] The next paper, a week older, told the rest of the story. Santiago had been hanged. The same day, disgraced and humiliated, Emily Greenwood had been found in the barn, hanging from the hayloft. (211–12)

These events began a feud which:

> led to the stabbing death of a Greenwood boy in the 1860s and the beating death of a Santiago in the second decade of the twentieth century. In the 1930s a minor war broke out that lasted nearly seven years, and took with it a half-dozen assorted Santiagos and Greenwoods, including one woman.
>
> In the years between there had been a host of lesser injuries, acts of vandalism, pranks and troubles.
>
> Including prison for Eli. (25–6)

Eli Santiago, the hero of the novel, fell in love with Sarah when they were both at high school and, after a secret affair, she found herself pregnant and they decided to marry. However, since Sarah's father was a police officer he was able to have Eli "charged [...] with statutory rape and alienation of affections. Garth Greenwood would have tried him for kidnapping, too, but someone talked sense into him" (38). The charges were "thrown out when he went before the judge" (38–9) but because Garth had "friends on the bench, friends all over" (134), Eli had been refused bail and had already "spent two months in jail waiting for his trial" (55). Sarah was "hauled away and hidden in a dreary, bleak home for unwed mothers [...] for nearly seven months" (109) until she had given birth and put her child up for adoption.

Sarah lost her baby but not her life, and Eli was charged with rape rather than hanged for it, but it is evident that the echoes of past events resonate down the centuries. That the story of the feud between the Greenwoods and the Santiagos is more than mere family history is indicated by the fact that Deborah Lucero, a historian who has already written a book "about Hispanic legends in the Southwest, [and] another about women in the Spanish colonial period" (220), considers the feud to be a part of "Hispanic history" (220). This is also evident in the way Eli frames his retelling of the tale:

> He leaned forward, donning an exaggerated Spanish accent. "Once upon a time, this land belonged to the descendants of the proud conquistadores, and their language and customs were Spanish, and all was well."
> Jennifer chuckled. "Except for the Indians."
> "Details," he said, waving them away. He smiled ruefully to let her know he was kidding. "Anyway, into this peaceful, abundant land came a horde of *americanos* who changed everything, took the land and changed the language, and would not go away. (59)

This is, as Eli states quite explicitly, "the romantic version" of the story told by his family rather than "the facts" (59). That acknowledgement, along with the "exaggerated" accent he adopts and his rueful smile, deliberately undercut this simplified narrative which erases the viewpoint and experiences of Native Americans; they indicate that both he and Wind are aware of the complexities of New Mexico's history. Furthermore, although the ethnicity of Wind's protagonists means that she, like Eli, is perforce focusing on interactions between Whites and Hispanics, her cast of characters in the present day includes Glenna O'Neal, a reference librarian, who is "a small, pretty black woman" (210) and Thomas Concha who has been Eli's "friend since high school" (152) and is "an Indian" (50). The novel's account of the events which took place in 1859 is even more closely focused on White and Hispanic characters but an indication that a significant proportion of New Mexico's population belonged to neither group is nonetheless provided via a couple of sentences which describe Emily Greenwood's father as "an avowed racist. Hated Indians and Mexicans and the blacks who were drifting in, a few at a time" (221).

The racism of one of Emily's brothers is evident in his "horrifying comment" (212) on his sister's suicide: "Like any decent woman, she didn't want to bring that mixed-race bastard into the world. At least this way, she'll have some peace" (212). Callous and bigoted though the statement was, the very strength of his abhorrence of miscegenation led to an unguarded choice of words which raises doubts about the veracity of a story which "had taken on the mythical power of a legend" (25) and, like the Myth of the Frontier, justifies the violence enacted by the "*americanos* who [...] took the land". His reference "to a specific child" (213) makes Sarah suspect that "Emily Greenwood had been a lot more than a week pregnant" (212), despite the rape allegedly having taken place only shortly before the hanging. Sarah is thus not wholly surprised to learn the facts discovered by Deborah Lucero, whose surname, appropriately enough, means "bright star". On the night Sarah visits her, Lucero shines a rigorous academic light on the old legend. She begins by warning Sarah that:

> "You may not like what I have found [...] But if you want truth, I will be happy to give it to you."
> Sarah took a breath. "I'm tired of the legends and the lies. I'd really like the truth." (214)

The truth, which Deborah Lucero discovered in "letters from Emily to a friend of hers in Philadelphia. I found them at the University of Pennsylvania archives when I did some background research into Emily's family" (222), is that Emily and Manuel were in love and "Manuel Santiago petitioned Emily's father for marriage three months before the hanging. Greenwood threw him out and threatened legal action if he came near his daughter again" (221).

Lucero's work, like that of many non-fictional American historians, demonstrates that violence was employed in order to maintain a racially "purified social contract" and that the myth created to justify this violence was "built on a lie" (235). The racism which made the lies more acceptable than the truth was still a powerful force when Sarah's parents were young: as Sarah's mother admits, "When we were children we never thought of mixing the way you all have. We stuck to our own" (50). Now, however, "Things are so different" (50) and perhaps because of this a truce can finally be reached between the two families: Garth Greenwood tells Eli " I can't promise I'll ever even like you, Eli Santiago, and I don't reckon you'll ever love me, either. [...] But I can respect you as a man" (242). Tentatively, a "new, purified social contract" seems to be emerging, built on truth, respect and compromise rather than on myths, conflict and a determination "to win the war" (Johnston 35).

The "long history of war between the families, a war that had eventually reduced two proud, wealthy families to nothing" (Wind 235) evidently brought neither side "regeneration". However, because Eli "chose to go another way—and because he did not become violent, as all his people and your people did before him" (187), he was able to break the cycle of destruction and instead start "a business that had made his family wealthy again, as they had not been in a hundred years" (201). It is a choice which supports the adage that "living well is the best revenge": the business benefited Eli while simultaneously infuriating his enemy, Garth Greenwood, who admits that "Every time I heard your name on television or saw it in the newspaper, I wanted to get out my gun and shoot you dead" (242).

In addition to repeatedly demonstrating to Garth Greenwood that he had not "done the right thing" (242) in separating Sarah and Eli, the latter's business:

> had benefited not only his own family; sixty-two people were employed permanently, with another thirty seasonally. And he did not think of it often, but he knew, somewhere in the back of his brain, that it was good for his *people* when an ordinary man made a success of things. He liked to think of some young boy, somewhere in the world, seeing an Hispanic name on a product and realizing that, he, too, could have a big dream. (201)

This hope, that the success of one member of a minority group can benefit all members of that group by serving as an encouragement and inspiration to them, is shared by the authors of some of the novels I examine in the next chapter.

The New Colossus

Here at our sea-washed, sunset gates shall stand
A mighty woman with a torch, whose flame
Is the imprisoned lightning, and her name
Mother of Exiles. [...]

"Keep ancient lands, your storied pomp!" cries she
With silent lips. "Give me your tired, your poor,
Your huddled masses yearning to breathe free.

—Emma Lazarus, "The New Colossus",
as inscribed at the base of the Statue of Liberty.

4. *E Pluribus Unum*: The Importance of Community

In Emma Barry's *Party Lines* (2015) a presidential candidate states that "The heart of our nation is that we rugged individualists are in it *together*". It is an insightful statement about a paradox at the core of American identity for although:

> many claim "rugged individualism" as the original hallmark of American character, any careful student of the development of the American nation will note the early and continued presence of communal values. (Durnbaugh 14)

Admittedly some, including Robert Putnam, author of the influential *Bowling Alone: The Collapse and Revival of American Community* (2000), would argue that in recent decades Americans "have been pulled apart from one another and from our communities" (27), but others take a far more positive view. Claude S. Fischer, for instance, has suggested that "the *voluntarism* that distinguished the culture of colonial America—a melding of individualism *with* community— seems to have strengthened and expanded over time" (ix). Indeed, the very success of Putnam's book can perhaps be read as an indication of the strength of the:

> emotive central appeal, particularly in the United States of America, of the fundamentally Christian narrative (paradise, the fall, the promise of redemption) that lies at the heart of Putnam's thesis: an idyllic and unified 'American community' of the past has, over the last thirty years, 'fallen' apart, and can be redeemed in the future only through a renewed commitment to civic participation and unity. (Arneil 2)

I have already argued (in the introduction) that one of romance novels' attractions for Americans is that they are redemption narratives. Another may be the fact that they place this redemption in the context of a community. Communities form the heart of romance fiction: at their smallest, they can be created by as few as two individuals who find love together, but they can expand outwards to incorporate a larger group, comprised of family and friends, the inhabitants of a town, or the citizens of a nation.

Linked romance novels, moreover, provide "readers with a greater sense of community than most individual novels" (Ramsdell 483) and it is perhaps no coincidence that since romance publishing's centre of gravity shifted from the UK to North America "the serial format has become increasingly prominent in the genre" (Goris). The "character-based" series creates a community because it is:

> structured around a group of recurring characters (siblings, colleagues, friends, inhabitants of a small town, etc.). Each installment in the series features the complete romance narrative of one member of the group. The narratives are connected to each other via the recurring characters and sometimes via non-romance subplots. (Goris)

This chapter will focus on two such series, Nora Roberts's The MacKades (1995–6) and Sharon Shinn's Twelve Houses series (2005–8), both of which depict the growth of romantic relationships against a backdrop of civil war, a type of military conflict that can rip apart communities on both a national and, often, a smaller, more familial scale.

Shinn had been made aware of readers' love of character-based series after discovering that:

> The thing that most people seemed to find disappointing about the Samaria books [an earlier series] was that they didn't follow the same people through successive storylines, so from the outset I planned the Twelve Houses books as a series about six main characters. ("Twelve Houses")

Although she is usually categorised as an author of sf/fantasy, Shinn has stated that, "while I try to layer on a lot of the fantastical elements of sf/f, and I certainly hope to provide a compelling plot, I usually think the love story is the core of the book" (Janine). Roberts, another American and "one of the most successful romance authors of all time, is often credited with being instrumental in popularizing the serial form in the romance genre" (Goris). Her novels about the MacKade brothers are set in contemporary Antietam, Maryland, which is, with the the exception of one or two of its inhabitants, an almost ideal, "close-knit community" (*The Fall* 117): it is "a good town, mostly a kind one. No one has to be alone here unless they want to" (*The Pride* 44). Nonetheless, it is literally haunted by the ghosts of the Civil War of 1861–5, which tore American society in two, and although the war's causes are not discussed in the series, its presence in the narrative serves as a constant reminder that communities can be destroyed as well as created. Shinn's series, by contrast, foregrounds a community's descent into civil war and it is only the final book in the series which provides glimpses of the magical kingdom of Gillengaria's recovery from civil strife. The two series thus complement each other, with Shinn's novels making clear the wider political implications of issues which are also present, albeit often less explicitly and usually with reference to personal relationships, in Roberts's series.

Destruction of Community

With regards to the destruction of community, the key factors are inequality, distrust, and violence.

1. Inequality

A great deal of evidence suggests that "inequality is divisive and socially corrosive" (Wilkinson and Pickett 195). Gillengaria's disintegration provides a fictional illustration of why this is so. It is a kingdom in which political and economic power is mainly in the hands of the "marlords," the heads of the:

> twelve noble Houses of Gillengaria—bloodlines and property
> divisions that have existed for centuries. Between them, they
> own virtually all the valuable land of the country. [...] They
> pretend to owe allegiance to the king, and generally they are
> loyal, but all of them believe that they are superior to royalty

and could rule much better if the chance fell to them. (Shinn,
Mystic 21–2)

Below them are the "Nobles and gentry who don't quite have the
pure bloodlines of the top families, but who possess wealth and
some prestige nonetheless" (61–2); "no matter which of the Twelve
Houses they hold allegiance to" (*Dark* 45), this group are "all lumped
under the rather derisive name of the Thirteenth House" *(Reader* 94).
Shinn does not describe the distinctions between the members of the
lower orders in as much detail, but both the peasantry and the urban
poor, who "know what it's like to grow up in poverty" (*Mystic* 137),
have representatives in the core group of characters in the persons
of Donnal, whose uncle is a "tenant farmer" (130), and Justin, who
spent his childhood in "the thieves' district" (137) of the royal city.

Gillengaria is, clearly, an extremely unequal society and although
many of the poor, including Donnal, seem content with their status,
there is some evidence that the vast differentials of power between
the richest and the poorest generate resentment in others: Justin
initially hates Kirra Danalustrous, another member of the group and
the daughter of a marlord, "for embodying all the rank and power of
a privileged, pampered class" (136).

2. Distrust

Inequality often leads to distrust. Those at the top of the social
hierarchy may fear reprisals from those beneath them in the social
hierarchy. As Justin remarks:

> There is a reason the very wealthy do not walk certain streets
> of the royal city unescorted. Boys like us would accost them
> in deep night or full daylight, and steal their purses and offer
> to take their lives. (*Mystic* 137)

Even their own homes cannot be deemed entirely safe, since "many a
servant has betrayed his lord" (*Thirteenth* 2). In Gillengaria, however,
the greater threat to the marlords and their families would appear to
derive from other nobles. Some of the marlords will lead the country
as a whole into war as they seek to overthrow the combined forces

of the king and the Houses loyal to the Crown. Against a backdrop
of growing unrest, the lesser, "Thirteenth House" nobility, are also
"growing restless" (79) as they tire "of being judged inferior. We
want equal voice, equal honours" (303); some "Thirteenth House
lords who have been dissatisfied with the distribution of property"
(*Reader* 243) eventually attack their Twelfth House overlords.

Those at the bottom of the social scale, meanwhile, are also likely
to be lacking in trust: "In virtually all societies 'have-nots' are less
trusting than 'haves,' probably because haves are treated by others
with more honesty and respect" (Putnam 138). This is shown to
be the case in both Roberts's and Shinn's fictional communities.
In Gillengaria the most oppressed minority group is comprised of
people with magical abilities. They are known as "mystics" and some
of them "had been beaten or threatened or abused so often that they
had little strength and no trust left in them" (Shinn, *Reader* 185).
Similarly, one of the heroines in Roberts's series, Savannah, lacks
trust; she still has a lot of strength but has nonetheless been marked by
the struggle to survive after her father "booted me out. I was sixteen,
and pregnant" (*The Pride* 43). Although she eventually succeeded in
making a career for herself as an illustrator, she is intensely aware that
she doesn't "have a fancy degree—hell, I don't have a high school
diploma" (241). Her early interactions with Regan, another heroine in
the series, demonstrate how, even inadvertently, "matters of taste and
class still keep people in their place—stopping them from believing
they can better their position and sapping their confidence if they try"
(Wilkinson and Pickett 164). In Regan, Savannah sees "elegance,
privilege and class" (Roberts, *The Pride* 119) and is reminded that
she doesn't "have any training" in art and knows "nothing of fine
antiques" (108). Her instinctive reaction is to leave Regan as fast as
she can, even though it means turning down a lucrative commission.

Savannah is equally quick to escape from the presence of Sheriff
Devin MacKade. Her instinctive distrust of him is unjustified, but
it is reasonable given her previous experience of people trying to
take her:

> baby away from me. [...] They tried. Social services, sheriffs,
> state cops. Whenever they could catch me, they tried. They

> wanted me in the system so they could tell me how to act, how
> to raise my child or, better for everyone, to give him away.
> (243)

A certain degree of distrust may also seem reasonable in the face of
the unknown, before the potential risk it poses has been fully assessed.
In Shinn's series, for example, Justin and Tayse "neither liked nor
trusted" (*Mystic* 10) Senneth initially, but their wariness was surely
justified given that at that point, "Her only true allegiances seemed to
be to herself and to her magic" (39) and she is an extremely powerful
mystic: "She *is* power [...]. She can do anything. She can create heat,
and light, and fire. [...] She can change shape if she wants to. She can
cast darkness" (13).

However, it is also possible for distrust to be less reasonable
and far more sinister: "Sometimes enemy groups are selected or
'created' by an emerging ideology, usually on the basis of cultural
devaluation, societal rifts, or real conflict" (Staub 61). In Gillengaria
the "emerging ideology" is that of the Daughters of the Pale Mother,
a sect led by Coralinda Gisseltess, who believe that "The mystics are
evil" (Shinn, *Mystic* 289). The Daughters have been "going around
proselytizing" (46), with the result that mystics have become deeply
feared and distrusted by the mass of the population even though the
majority of them:

> have such small skills. They can—change themselves—or
> heal someone else's cut—or maybe read someone else's emo-
> tion. They can't—they can't fight with their power. They can't
> hurt anyone. (31)

The non-mystics, however, are more than capable of harming those
they distrust.

3. Violence

While it seems that "Mystics have never been entirely safe" (Shinn,
Mystic 170) from violence, Coralinda and her brother Halchon have
intentionally "laid the foundation of faith and fear, by spreading hatred
of the mystics and promoting the sanctity of the Pale Mother" (181)

in order vastly to increase the acceptability, severity and frequency of the violence and destabilise the kingdom. As the series begins, tales are spreading:

> of mystics hunted down in the middle of the night, and turned out in the streets—or worse [...] there have been—deaths— murders—terrible stories of mystics who have been found mutilated in their own homes. (46)

This violence is the result of a campaign of terror orchestrated by Coralinda and Halchon, whose troops roam the countryside intent on the destruction of mystics. There are, moreover, rumours that the Queen is a mystic and:

> you can imagine how this scenario plays [...]. 'The queen is a mystic! She has ensnared the king in her spells! We must trample all mystics and depose the king, and make Gillengaria safe again!' (180)

Unlike his sister, who believes that the destruction of the king is "the task the Pale Mother has given me" (291), Halchon's primary motivation is "to rule the country" (362) but he admits that "My sister's passion has been convenient [...] We pursue the same ends for different reasons" (363). They also pursue them by the same violent methods.

Since Halchon's ambitions are thwarted before he can ascend the throne, one cannot be certain how he would have acted as ruler of the entire kingdom. His ruthless pursuit of power, however, suggests that he would have made "a bad king—unjust and violent" (*Reader* 314). All the indications are that under his rule Gillengaria would have become a "predatory society" in which:

> there is no real community, no shared commitment to any common vision of the public good, and no respect for law. [...] People ally with one another in the quest for power and privilege, but not as equals. Rather, relations are steeply hi- erarchical. [...] Blatant inequalities in power and status cu- mulate into vertical chains of dependency and exploitation, secured by patronage and coercion. (Diamond 298)

Such an outcome might also be predicted on the basis of his personality if, like one of the minor characters in Shinn's series, one believes that:

> the personality of an overlord was always reflected in the attitudes of those who served him. A bad master bred vicious men; a weak ruler spawned anxious and opportunistic subjects. A good king, by contrast, created an environment of prosperity, and his people were successful, content, satisfied, and inclined to peace. (Shinn, *Reader* 2)

The extent of the correlation between good politics and good personal morals is debatable, but it is certainly true that the destruction Halchon is prepared to wreak on his community finds a parallel in the deeply negative nature of his relationships with his wife, Sabina, and with Senneth, whom he would like to marry. Halchon has the "ability to dampen or disarm magic. [...] Around him, Senneth became mortal and powerless and weak" (*Thirteenth* 291). For Senneth, the freedom to practice magic is akin to the "Freedom of ethnic, religious, racial, and other minority groups [...] to practice their religion and culture" (Diamond 22). Marriage to Halchon would therefore be deeply damaging to Senneth even were it not for the fact that in such a union she would be unlikely to enjoy the democratic right to "equality [...] under a rule of law" (Diamond 22). Halchon appears to view a wife as an asset to be disposed of when she becomes inconvenient and Sabina has felt "frightened and wholly alone" for "the entire sixteen years" (Shinn, *Thirteenth* 340) of her marriage. In contrast to the situation in an optimally functioning democratic society, where all citizens enjoy "Substantial individual freedom of belief, opinion, discussion, speech" (Diamond 22), when Sabina wishes to discuss the political situation with Senneth they have to meet surreptitiously because it puts Sabina "in very grave danger" (Shinn, *Thirteenth* 340). Given that the latter seems to have "spent the entire span of her marriage in a heightened state of readiness, prepared for the next insult, the next blow, the next threat against her life" (*Dark* 242), it could be said that she has lacked "freedom [...] from torture, terror, and unjustified detention" (Diamond 22).

The destructive, "predatory" community embodied in the relationship between Sabina and Halchon Gisseltess finds its parallel in Roberts's series in that between Cassie and Joe Dolin. Like Sabina, Cassie has spent over a decade tied to an abusive husband and both women make the decision to leave for very similar reasons: Sabina fled from Halchon after overhearing him "tell his sister that the time had come to do away with her" (Shinn, *Dark* 245); Cassie walked out after an incident in which Joe "choked her until she accepted that he would kill her" (Roberts, *The Return* 76). Joe's extreme brutality on this occasion was prompted by his having been fired from his job "because he went to work drunk and mouthed off to his supervisor" (76); "he came home and took it out on" (76) Cassie. This chain of events illustrates the connection between inequality and violence and, although it is on a domestic scale, the same dynamic often plays out on a larger stage too:

> When people react to a provocation from someone with higher status by redirecting their aggression on to someone of lower status, psychologists label it *displaced aggression*. Examples include: the man who is berated by his boss and comes home and shouts at his wife and children; [...] the ways in which people in deprived communities react to an influx of foreign immigrants. (Wilkinson and Pickett 166–7)

Joe had always compensated for his lower status at work by ensuring that in the domestic sphere his status was far superior to Cassie's. Even in the earliest days of their marriage he insisted on his economic superiority: although Cassie worked, Joe would declare that "I earn the money in my house. I don't need no woman paying my way" (Roberts, *The Return* 10). He evidently thinks himself to be superior by virtue of his gender and, in addition, believes that "A woman belongs to her husband" (183) and is "his property" (*The Heart* 68). Furthermore, in his mind the marriage contract legitimates violence: "A man had a right to punish his wife, to give her the back of his hand or let her feel his fist when she needed it" (68).

This inevitably left Cassie "wary of a man's strength" (24) but in spite of her distrust of men, over the course of the series she becomes romantically involved with Devin MacKade, from whom she demands and receives "trust and respect" (200). This new relationship is, in some ways, the mirror image of her old one. Devin is "rough, she supposed. She knew he could break up a bar fight with little more than a snarl, and that he used his fists when that didn't work" (39) but, unlike Joe, he does not use violence to oppress or terrorise others, whether in the context of an intimate relationship or in that of the community as a whole. As sheriff, he is in a position of power and authority but whereas Joe used his power to hurt and oppress others, Devin uses his "to serve the town, protect its citizens. Not to relieve his own bitter frustrations" (*The Return* 91). Finally, although he is a man who has what some might consider "a real man's job" (*The Heart* 33), he himself was taught well by a mother who "didn't believe there was women's work and men's work" (*The Return* 65–6) and so he has no interest in enforcing rigid gender roles or denigrating women. With him, Cassie knows she would not be treated as an inferior, nor would she need to fear violence and so she resolves to:

> teach herself not to be so jittery around Devin. [...] She would stop thinking of how big his hands were, or what would happen if he got angry and used them against her. (*The Heart* 39)

Roberts's series therefore demonstrates that making the transition from a destructive relationship characterised by inequality, distrust and violence, to a supportive and positive one is difficult but possible.

Restoration of Community

Shinn's series shows how whole communities can make a similar journey and the key factors in ensuring a transition to a happier, more inclusive community, would appear to be respect, "generalised reciprocity", and negotiation.

Negotiation

Senneth, and the royal house for which she often acts as an ambassador, are characterised by a willingness to negotiate in good faith and a disinclination to resort to violence and coercion. The vast difference between the forces of the predatory society and those of constructive civic engagement are illustrated when, on the eve of war, Senneth insists that "we need to take one last chance to try to bargain with" Halchon (Shinn, *Reader* 317). The latter agrees to a meeting but it ends with a carefully orchestrated surprise attack by his troops because Halchon's preference was to kill all his opponents "if he could [...], even though he had agreed to parley in peace" (324).

Clearly, negotiation cannot create a better society unless it is successful, and this is not always the case. It is often a slow, painstaking process which can be overtaken by events: King Baryn's negotiations with members of the Thirteenth House, for instance, progressed well but were not sufficient to stave off war or save his life. They did, nonetheless, provide the basis for a compromise agreed after the conclusion of the war:

> It had fallen to his daughter, Amalie, and her various advisors to craft a scheme to divide and apportion properties, but over the past two years, the plan had been worked out. Now there were Twelve Houses and Twenty-Four Manors, and any number of confusing but jealously guarded titles. (*Fortune* 12)

Such changes may not have "brought down, leveled at once" (*Reader* 364) all the barriers of class in Gillengaria, but they do go some way towards making it a less unequal society.

Respect

One of the most important preconditions for successful negotiation is respect:

> if people (and parties and interest groups) with sharply different goals and beliefs are going to be able to bargain and compromise, they have to respect one another. That requires tolerance of political, ethnic, racial, and other differences. (Diamond 156)

This type of respect, based not on fear of the other's power but on appreciation for, or at least tolerance of, their differences, is the kind of respect which Princess Amalie wishes to foster in her kingdom.

She couches her argument in terms of magic and theology:

> I believe *all* magic flows from the gods—and I believe there
> are many gods and goddesses that the people of Gillengaria
> have long forgotten. [...] Not only that, I believe all of us have
> been touched by the gods to some degree. (Shinn, *Reader* 438)

Her uncle, the regent, uses more prosaic language but shows a similar
respect for others as he tries "to see every man as my equal—perhaps
not in intelligence, perhaps not in wealth, but having some knowledge
or some skill that I do not possess" (Shinn, *Thirteenth* 49). This is
an attitude shared by Jared MacKade, who "says everybody's got a
special talent [...] everybody's got something inside that makes him
different" (Roberts, *The Pride* 124).

   In Shinn's series the respect shown to others by the leaders of
the new regime even extends to views it finds abhorrent: "Amalie
feels we will be unable to expect tolerance for mystics if we show
intolerance for a group that despises them" (Shinn, *Fortune* 164). Her
position indicates an expectation that, for good or for ill, people will
tend to reciprocate the treatment they themselves are offered.

Generalised Reciprocity

Respect and goodwill can often be generated, and distrust dissipated,
by acts of kindness, as when Kirra uses her mystical powers to heal
a burns victim:

> "Thank you. I did not realize—I could not have expected—
> thank you for your kindness. I will never curse your people
> again. [...] I will do a kindness someday for a mystic if I can."
> "Then I am repaid." (Shinn, *Thirteenth* 281)

This is just one of the occasions on which Shinn's series provides
support for the concept of "paying it forward", which is very similar
to:

> the principle of generalized reciprocity—I'll do this for you
> now, without expecting anything immediately in return and
> perhaps without even knowing you, confident that down the
> road you or someone else will return the favor. (Putnam 134)

Indeed, the very first chapter of the first book opens with Senneth rescuing Cammon, a young mystic who, it transpires, has the ability to read others' emotions: over the course of the series he returns the favour many times over by alerting the others to danger.

Another of Senneth's acts of generalised reciprocity teaches the principle to someone else. Justin had hitherto only been aware of one-to-one reciprocity, in which people act to help others in the knowledge that it will benefit them directly, as when "The strong take care of the powerful so that the powerful can take care of them in turn" (Shinn, *Mystic* 223). It therefore both deeply "impressed Justin" to see "someone strong fight for someone weak [...] Just *because* the weak one has no other defenders" (223) and "changed him" (Shinn, *Dark* 234) into the kind of person who would also carry out acts of generalised reciprocity.

His first such act, albeit less disinterested than Senneth's, because he had thought "he might win an ally" (Shinn, *Dark* 79), brings him into contact with his future wife. Ellynor "would have been grateful to anyone for such a service" (74) but Justin particularly appeals to her because of his subsequent:

> attitude [...]. He had accompanied her [...] because he wanted her to be safe, not because he thought she was incapable of caring for herself. Because he valued her, not because he distrusted her.
>
> And he had talked to her as equal to equal, seeming to be unaware of any gulfs that might be caused by gender, social status, or intellect. (74–5)

His respect for her expresses itself most fully, perhaps, in his willingness to negotiate with her:

> He was powerful enough, he knew, to restrain her—now, and anytime in the future when she considered a course of action he did not like. [...] Which made it doubly important that he not impose his will on her. (379–80)

When Justin's arguments fail to convince Ellynor he, like the parties who lose an election in a stable democracy, respects her decision rather than resorting to violence in order to change the outcome.

Theirs, then, is a romantic relationship which demonstrates that respect, negotiation, and generalised reciprocity can also lay the foundations for a successful community on a more personal level.

Growing the Successful Community

The success of the micro-community formed by a romance's protagonists is often made manifest in the form of a baby. Justin and Ellynor, for instance, have a one-year-old daughter in the final book of Shinn's series. She is not, however, merely her parents' daughter: Ellynor's large extended family are also "excited to see Ceribel" (*Fortune* 131). Similarly, in Roberts's series it is clear that a baby born to any one of the MacKade couples is "a MacKade baby, and would belong to all of them" (*The Pride* 172). If a baby can expand the communities formed by couples and their extended families, it may also function, at least in part, as a symbolic promise of a happy future for the family's wider community because, as the mystic Aleatha asks, "What is a baby but hope, after all?" (Shinn, "When Winter" 125).

Both series make clear that community is not created solely through the expansion of the biological family. Before Jared MacKade proposes to Savannah, he asks her son "to take my name [...]. And to take me on, as your father" (Roberts, *The Pride* 239). Later, when Devin MacKade asks Cassie to marry him, he does so while holding her:

> children as if they were already his.
> Of course, they were. (*The Heart* 250)

Roberts's series thus suggests that, as Devin MacKade puts it, "Family isn't just blood" (26). This is a conclusion which can also be drawn from Shinn's series. In the course of their travels together, Senneth, Tayse, Kirra, Donnal, Cammon and Justin slowly form a "small, strangely bound group" (*Thirteenth* 321). On learning that Cammon is an orphan, Kirra declares "We'll be your family now" (*Mystic* 136) and, in turn, Tayse treats "Kirra like an impulsive and reckless younger sister" (*Reader* 70). Justin too has lost his biological family and as Senneth observes, "More than any of us [...] considers the rest of us to be his family" (*Thirteenth* 371). Tayse is a "father" (*Dark* 449) to him and Senneth too is "kin" (441) "though we are not related by blood and we have not formally adopted each other" (461). The other three take the place of Justin's lost siblings: when asked to define her relationship with him, Kirra replies "He's my brother" (364); he and Donnal work "together like jealous brothers, understanding each other even when their dislike was at its strongest" (*Thirteenth* 46); he treats Cammon "like a younger brother of whom he was inordinately fond" (*Mystic* 382).

"Other" Communities

Strong, supportive, communities can be found in a great many American romance novels, with settings as diverse as: Ellison, Iowa, which holds "county fairs and ice cream socials" (T. Weir 186) and "where all the residents knew one another's religious preferences, bank account numbers and birthdays" (30); the aristocratic nineteenth-century English milieu inhabited by families such as Julia Quinn's Bridgertons; a Scotland populated by "heroic warriors, sexy and dedicated to clan and family" (Hague and Stenhouse 361); isolated Montana ranches where "the [...] personnel simulate both a multigenerational family and a small community" (Cook 68); and businesses in which the employees "have extremely close (often familial) ties with their employers" (Young 100). Some readers, like the eponymous heroine of Theresa Weir's *Loving Jenny* (1989) before her arrival in the small close-knit community of Ellison, may believe the more idyllic of these communities could exist only in an "idealistic writer's imagination" (172) but their popularity suggests that romance author Courtney Milan is hardly alone in finding romances:

> valuable not just for the romantic relationship, but for the value that they place on community and friendship and be- longing. In our world, it's so easy to just disappear and be alone, and it's always important to have the reminder that no matter how bad things seem, it will always be better with good friends and family. (qtd. in Wendell 161)

The communities depicted in romances, however, may not be ones with which all romance readers can identify or in which they can vicariously feel a sense of belonging.

Suzanne Juhasz has argued that it is a "common readerly desire to identify with literary plots and characters—to achieve the satisfaction and also the instruction that derive from the process of seeing oneself depicted in fiction" (67). Although romances do provide many readers with this experience, which the heroine of Rose Lerner's *In for a Penny* (2010) describes as producing a "spark of recognition" and the feeling "that here was *myself*" (72), a substantial proportion of romance readers cannot often find either that spark or that feeling in mainstream romances. Beverly Jenkins, for example, who is now a famous African-American romance author, grew up reading mainstream historical romantic novels which apparently failed to produce the desired "spark":

> Not a one featured [or even included] women who looked like us, but as we read them we longed for stories that did feature us, stories that reflected the love our parents shared or our grand-parents shared; the love that we saw in that married couple at church who was always holding hands; or the love we see every time we look into our partner's eyes. (Osborne 2021)

Clearly, Black readers were and are able to enjoy novels featuring White protagonists; in 1992 Leslie Wainger, Senior Editor of Silhouette Intimate Moments, recalled the many letters she had received from readers who identified themselves variously "as black, […] as a woman of color, [...] as an African-American. […] Always my correspondent tells me that she enjoys our books anyway" (McGill 2). Nonetheless, as Wainger acknowledged in her introductory letter to readers of Joyce McGill's *Unforgivable* (1992), the first romance in her line to feature an African-American hero and heroine, only the publication of such a novel could give:

> all of us a chance to prove what the sages have told us down through the years: Love is indeed blind. It recognizes no boundaries of color, of country, of language or of age. Love is always love, and all of us can share in its bounty. (McGill 2)

When salient characteristics of romance readers' identities are consistently absent from the identities of the novels' protagonists, the cumulative effect is to suggest that those characteristics would debar readers who possessed them from attaining a truly romantic "happy ending" of their own.

The lack may also be felt to erase, or minimise the importance of, those readers' communities. Certainly the converse can be true. Lynn S. Neal, for instance, argues that a large part of historical "inspirational" romance novels':

> appeal to [...] readers comes from learning or imagining that women like them, with moral and religious values like theirs, comprised an important part of historical events. Through these narratives, evangelical readers can claim a central place for themselves in the past and in the present, in the United States and in the world. (177–8)

Lesbian readers of lesbian romance novels would also seem to be seeking a "place for themselves" which validates their importance. According to Karin Kallmaker, an author of lesbian romance novels:

> lesbian romance stories are the only novels where a woman can go to find affirmation of her hopes, her dreams and her choices in life. They reflect and celebrate the evolving nature of our relationships, friendships and community. ("Why")

This is, of course, a very bold claim but lesbian romances certainly are, as stated by one of the secondary characters in Kallmaker's *In Every Port* (1989), "a trifle more self-affirming" (75) than the classic *The Well of Loneliness* (1928) which, "Jokingly, and not so jokingly, [...] became known as 'the Bible of lesbianism'. For a good four decades it held undisputed sway as *the* lesbian novel" (Hennegan viii). Jessica, one of Kallmaker's protagonists, therefore puts *The Well* back on the shelf and instead buys Jane Rule's *Desert of the Heart* (1964), "a gentle romance" (Schuster 433) which ends on a note of "warm affirmation" (436) and *Patience and Sarah* (1969), by Isabel Miller, which "follows, on the whole, a typical romance trajectory" (Palmer 190) and concludes on the requisite optimistic note. Jessica finds these "two books [...] inspiring and stirring" (Kallmaker, *In*

Every 81), buys more, and consequently "discovered her feminism again. She was interested in politics again" (81).

In Every Port might have a similarly stimulating effect itself if the reader is encouraged to emulate Jessica and recognise that "I'm not free from the world and responsibilities to my—kind" (74). It is a sentiment echoed in Beverly Jenkins's historical African-American romance *Belle* (2002) in which the hero's mother affirms her support for the heroine, Belle, by explaining that "We must help each other if we are all to move forward" (75). Both novels could be described as consciousness-raising romances: they bear witness to the history of the group to which the protagonists and the intended reader belong, and seem to urge the latter to show solidarity with others in that group.

Kallmaker's novel is set in 1978 against a backdrop of anti-gay activism and the assassination of Harvey Milk, whom Kallmaker describes in an author's note as "the first martyr of my generation" (217). Jenkins's *Belle*, set in 1859, packs in even more historical details, in this case about the history of abolitionism and prominent members of the African-American community at the time. Jenkins even includes a bibliography of her sources in case "this book has made you curious about [...] historical aspects of Belle's story" (248). She has stated elsewhere that she feels "it's been my ministry [...] to bring that 19th century to life in a way that people can access it, people can be proud of who they were" (Kahn 2). An additional argument in favour of learning about the past can be found in the novel itself given that the hero's mother:

> says education is crucial to one's upbringing—that and know-ing the history of our people. [...] Because we can't tell others about our accomplishments if we don't know them ourselves. (Jenkins 25)

Both romances explicitly intertwine the personal and the political because although:

> Finding one's heart's desire, as required by the romantic nar-rative, takes precedence, [...] Kallmaker emphasizes that the couple belongs to a wider world and has a responsibility to ac-knowledge that relationship as well as the private. (Betz 151)

In *Belle* the link between romantic fulfilment and political activism is, if anything, even closer. Daniel, the hero, makes a decision to break with his intended, Francine, in large part because of her lack of political engagement. Over time, he finds that they are:

> butting heads more and more often over his commitment to the Cause. Francine had been free all of her life. [...] [S]he [...] didn't give a hoot about abolitionism or its ancillary issues. [...] She'd much rather Daniel spend his time taking her shopping [...] than waste the day away setting the groundwork for political rallies or distributing broadsides. (Jenkins 65–6)

In contrast, Belle has been personally affected by slavery, she left her first abolitionist rally "determined to do all she could to help aid the cause" (151) and Daniel knows she would therefore make a good "helpmate, a supporter of her husband's life, not ... fussing because he preferred working for the Cause to shopping" (166).

Both romances are set in an oppressive political context which attempts to frame the protagonists, and people like them, as inferior. The "proposal sponsored by State Senator John Briggs to save the country's children by barring any homosexual person from teaching in public schools" (Kallmaker, *In Every* 10) clearly implies that lesbians such as Jessica are a threat to children while Daniel finds himself "living in a country whose constitution counted him as three-fifths of a person" (Jenkins 58–9). To make matters worse, in the:

> Supreme Court's 1858 decision in the Dred Scott case [...] Justice Taney had [...] written that members of the race were so inferior in the eyes of the Constitution that "they had no rights which a White man was bound to respect." (57)

These injustices are set to persist after the novel's conclusion, as is the "Fugitive Slave Act of 1850" which allows slave catchers to seize any African-American "they choose, slave or free" (36). Although in Kallmaker's novel a note of optimism is struck by the defeat of the Briggs amendment, the assassination of Harvey Milk indicates that here too, as in *Desert of the Heart*, "threats continue to menace [the protagonists] from an outside order that remains powerful" (Schuster 435).

In Kallmaker's *In Every Port*, as in Jenkins's *Belle*, the key group scenes are ones which symbolise the struggle that lies ahead for the protagonists' community as it seeks equality with the rest of society. This is in contrast to many mainstream romances, in which a triumphant note is struck by a group:

> scene or scenes [in which] the promised wedding is depicted, or some other celebration of the new community is staged, such as a dance or a fete […]. Society has reconstituted itself around the new couple(s) and the community comes together to celebrate this. (Regis, *A Natural* 38)

In Kallmaker's novel there is no wedding scene and the novel concludes instead with the heroines expressing their grief at the assassination of Harvey Milk by joining a march:

> At first there were just those who started in Castro. Gay men and women […]. Kind candlelight illuminated faces torment-ed with despair and grief. […] As they left Castro the crowd began to swell, began to change. Now there were older peo-ple, heterosexual couples, all carrying candles. […] Did it take death, pain, suffering to bring people together? (214–15)

As the heroines head for home together, the bitter-sweet answer to that question would seem to be that often it does, and the implication is there will be much more suffering before "gay and lesbian people" are fully accepted as part of US society and never "looked at […] as if we were insects" (193). One can draw similar conclusions from the most significant crowd scenes in Jenkins's novel. In this book there is in fact a scene depicting the promised wedding but only because after the novel was first published (under the title *Belle and the Beau*) "many readers […] wanted to know if Belle and Daniel actually married, so I took that into consideration this time around" (248). The most dramatic crowd scene, however, and one which was present in the original, towards the end of the novel, takes place on the day Belle has chosen as her birthday "Because on August first, 1834, the British freed [...] slaves in the West Indies. It was the beginning of slavery's end in Great Britain" (180). As the community are gathered just over the border in Canada in order to mark the anniversary, American slave catchers attempt to reclaim some escaped slaves. Appropriately given the day's British associations, their "writ […] from the sovereign state of Georgia" (223) is invalid on "land [which] belongs to Her Majesty Queen Victoria" (225) and it is the slave catchers themselves who are led off into captivity. It is a joyful event, in which "abolitionist men, Black and White" (223) cooperate to defeat their foes, but it is, nonetheless, one which cannot resolve the underlying political issues that face the African-American community in the US.

Conclusion

The US is a diverse nation; its romantic fiction reflects that diversity. US romance novels thus implicitly and explicitly reveal deep political divisions in American society. Nonetheless, American popular romance fiction, like a textual Statue of Liberty, holds aloft a beacon of hope: as "Mother of Exiles" she offers her readers the promise of community. Whether it will be fulfilled for individual readers may depend on whether they can find novels which evoke that "spark of recognition" and the feeling "that here was *myself*" (Lerner 72). For some, these books may be found not in the mainstream of popular romance fiction but in sub-genres such as African-American, 'inspirational' and lesbian romance. Nonetheless, by flourishing and showing increasing diversity in the face of a society which "labels the books as trash and the readers as unintelligent, uneducated, unsophisticated, or neurotic" (Krentz, "Introduction" 1), US romance fiction cries with silent lips to the guardians of high culture that they may keep their storied pomp. She welcomes her much maligned masses of readers and responds to the hopes and fears of the uprooted.

Tumbleweed

"Tumbleweeds lodged against a Wire Fence in Winter"
from Joseph Y. Bergen's *Foundations of Botany*

5. Roots

Oscar Handlin declared in the opening pages of *The Uprooted* (1951) that: "Once I thought to write a history of the immigrants in America. Then I discovered that the immigrants *were* American history" (3). Even leaving aside "American history" prior to the founding of Jamestown in 1607, it has been observed that Handlin's:

> narrative can only be maintained at the expense of understanding what is *not* part of a process of immigration in the growth of territory and peoples in American history: the slave trade; slavery; segregation; the internal conquest and settler colonialism by which the Native Americans were subdued and southwestern lands and their Mexican population were incorporated into the United States; and the international imperialism through which Filipinos, Puerto Ricans, and Pacific Islanders came under the control of the United States. (Gerber 5)

However, many of the individuals affected by these processes, while not "immigrants" of the kind featured in Handlin's history, could, nonetheless, also be described as "uprooted", as could many of those caught up in "environment-related population movements" such as "The Dust Bowl migration and migration responses to Hurricane Katrina" (McLeman 412).

Given that, as the previous two chapters have demonstrated, US romance novels not infrequently show their characters uprooting themselves or mention their characters' biological or geographic "roots" or lack of them, I realised I could not conclude my exploration of the politics of US romance without discussing Americans' experiences of uprootedness. In addition to having "uprooted" ancestors, many Americans will have direct experience of being "uprooted" themselves: according to Handlin "No one moves without sampling something of the immigrants' experience" (6). Research published in 2008 suggests that over "six-in-ten adults (63%) have moved to a new community at least once in their lives" and almost a quarter of "U.S.-born adults (23%) say the place they consider home in their heart isn't where they're living now" (Cohn and Morin 1). Obviously, this does mean that many "uprooted" individuals would consider their current residence their "heart home", like the fictional Addie Stapleton who has worked so hard to fit in to her new hometown that:

> Nobody remembered that Addie hadn't always been part of the community, and that suited her fine. If she'd had her way, she would have been born and raised among these people and their modest homes and businesses. Too bad the good Lord didn't give a body the choice of where to come into the world. Roots were important to Addie, and she had sunk hers deep here in Van Caster. (St. John 12)

They may be deep, but Addie's musings suggest they would be deeper had she "been born and raised among these people" and perhaps deeper still had her ancestors "been born and raised" there too.

Roots with this type of depth are possessed by Nora Roberts's Shane MacKade, Sharon Shinn's Malcolm Danalustrous, and Ruth Wind's Eli Santiago. Shane is a farmer who has always known:

> The land was his. He'd felt that in his bones, as long as he could remember. As if at birth someone had whispered it in his ear. […] The land his father had worked, and his father before that. And before that. (Roberts, *The Fall* 11–12)

A Gillengarian aristocrat, Malcolm can no doubt trace his ancestry back for generations and his "mystical connection" to his land is so deep he can "feel every footstep as it falls on Danalustrous soil" (Shinn, *Reader* 236). As for Eli, he lives where the:

> land calmed him. It always had. He was as intimate with these views, this light, these hills, these fields as he was with his own body. And it was not just his own memory and knowledge, but that of his father and grandfather and great-great-great-grandfather before him, all those men who had lived here and walked here for generations. (Wind 24)

All three have extremely deep roots; their knowledge of, and sense of connection to, their forebears and the land set them apart from the many Americans who, by heredity or personal circumstances, have been "uprooted".

It is difficult to know exactly how many Americans feel "uprooted" but evidently a considerable number do. With African-American "roots-tourists" in mind:

> In 2003 the government [of Ghana] founded the Ministry of Tourism and Diasporan Relations. Genealogy-related tourism in Ghana has contributed a significant boost to the tourist economy. Ghana focuses on ancestral tourism through its so-called 'roots packages'. Even though these packages are aimed at the African diaspora worldwide, the African American market counts for the greatest part of those who make the return visits. (Fehler 589)

Karyn Langhorne's *Street Level: An Urban Fairytale* (2005), concludes with her heroine, Thea, making this type of journey along with her hero and her son: they are on board a plane flying towards "the continent of Africa, soil of their ancestors and her one true home" (376). In addition, "some genealogy records from before the Civil War" provide evidence that Thea is "the great-great-great granddaughter of some African queen" (366). This latter element of the narrative could simply be ascribed to the fact that Thea, who somewhat sarcastically described herself as a "Ghetto Cinderella" (9) in the opening pages of the novel, is the protagonist of a work explicitly labelled an "urban fairytale": it seems apt that at the end of the tale she, like Cinderella, should be a princess. However, it would also seem to tap in to one of the "ideological narratives of U.S. black nationalist imaginaries that took shape in the mid-1960s and continue[s] to circulate in the present" (Clarke 73). This is the "African nobility narrative", which:

> By highlighting the idea that African Americans are not merely victims of slavery but descendants of an African noble and religious elite who are, at the present time, culturally imprisoned in the racist United States, [...] ambitiously links the no-

ble African past with African American hopes for an institu-
tionally empowered future. (Clarke 73–74)

This narrative thus uses newly-discovered roots to help uprooted
Americans grow tall and vigorous in the land to which they were
transplanted.

Research into roots, then, has the potential to empower an
individual and give them pride in their ancestors but it can also, as the
mention of African-Americans' forebears being "victims of slavery"
suggests, reveal painful links to the US's racist and often violent past.
When one White heroine replies enviously to a hero with Comanche
paternal ancestors and Irish maternal ones that:

> "My family is typical American mongrel. It must be won-
> derful to know something about your ancestors."
>
> Cody's mouth twisted. Wonderful. Yes, he was proud of his
> heritage, but he'd never have used the word "wonderful." He
> thought of his grandfather, clinging to the remnants of a cul-
> ture that had all but died before he was born, and of his father
> desperately trying to deny his heritage. And his mother, trying
> to bridge the gap between her background and her husband's.
>
> No, "wonderful" was not quite the term he would have
> used. (Schulze 94)

While non-White roots may have a bitter-sweet flavour, in which
pride is mixed with pain and anger, White roots may be a source of
guilt or shame.

Psychologists have suggested that "when people feel a strong
attachment to their group, they are motivated to search for and
use methods of avoiding feelings of guilt about their group's past
behavior" (Doosje *et al* 326). An example of this can be found in
Joan Domning's *The Forever Man* (1993), in which the heroine,
Carla Hudson, has to abandon her belief that "The first Hudson came
from Ohio and grubbed the ranch out with honest sweat" (26): he
took it from Nick Leclerc's "great-great-grandfather, [Frenchman]
Pierre Leclerc, [...] a fur trapper [...] married [to] a Flathead Indian
woman" (25). Moreover, the reason that "first Hudson" appropriated
the land was because of:

a love affair between Pierre's son, Michel, and the settler's daughter, Emily. [...] It was acceptable for trappers and settlers to cavort with Indian women, but they frowned upon the products of those relationships nosing around their daughters. *That*'s why Pierre and his family were booted out. (27)

Carla begins by denying the truth and then, having accepted it, attempts to stop Nick making a movie, based on the story, which will make it more widely known that her ancestor was "a *dishonest bigot!*" (28). A non-fictional example of a similar reaction is the statement:

released [...] on Facebook, which read: "I didn't want any television show about my family to include a guy who owned slaves. I was embarrassed. The very thought left a bad taste in my mouth. [...]". (Kasperkevic)

That was written in April 2015 by the Hollywood actor and director Ben Affleck, after he had unsuccessfully attempted to prevent the details of his ancestor's slave-owning past becoming public knowledge.

There may, then, be certain psychological advantages, if White, to having somewhat shorter roots in the US. Descent from immigrants:

who came ashore in the United States as "free white persons" under the terms of reigning naturalization law, yet whose racial credentials were not equivalent to those of the Anglo-Saxon "old stock" (Jacobson, *Whiteness* 3–4)

allows an individual to state that their ancestors "never *saw* an Indian. They came to this country after that. Nor were they responsible for enslaving the blacks (or anyone else)" (Novak xliv). Furthermore, for some this sort of ancestry might be considered grounds on which to "disavow any participation in [...] white privilege on the spurious basis of their parents' and grandparents' racial oppression" (Jacobson, *Whiteness* 7). Or, to state the matter even more strongly:

ethnic self-distancing from whiteness and privilege [...] fossilizes racial injustice in dim national antiquity, and so glosses over more recent discriminatory practices in housing, hiring, and unionization, for instance, which *did* benefit these

"newcomers," fresh off the boat though they were. (Jacobson,
Roots 22)

According to Mary C. Waters, a sociologist studying Americans'
ethnic identities, "The degree of intermarriage [...] among whites
of European extraction in the United States means that they enjoy a
great deal of choice and numerous options when it comes to ethnic
identification" (16). It is possible, therefore, that a wish to absolve
themselves of inherited responsibility for historic racial oppression
may be one factor explaining why, "When given a choice among
European ancestries, the more recent, more 'ethnic' of the groups"
were chosen by the "third- and fourth-generation [...] whites of
European extraction" she interviewed in 1986–87 (36, 11–12).

By contrast Scottish-Americans, in the words of the US Senate's
1998 resolution declaring 6 April to be National Tartan Day,
"successfully helped shape this country in its formative years and
guide this Nation through its most troubled times" (qtd. in Hague,
"The Scottish" 140). In recent years many Americans have been
proudly claiming Scottish roots; "celebration of Scottish roots has
been on the rise since the 1980s" (Satterwhite 326). In the 1990s the
"number of Highland Games and Scottish Festivals held in the United
States doubled [...] to over two hundred per year with events being
held in almost every state" (Hague and Stenhouse 360). In addition to
US-based activities which seek to connect Scottish-Americans with
their roots, there has also been a growth in "roots-tourism":

> Indeed, so significant has 'roots-tourism' become [...] that the
> Scottish Executive has identified it as a key 'niche market'
> deserving of capital investment to encourage its development.
> (Basu 151)

Americans make up a significant proportion of the 'roots-tourists'
who visit Scotland: in 2012 there were thought to be 0.5 million
Americans "interested in finding out more about their ancestry and
planning to visit Scotland in the next two years" (Tourism Intelligence
Scotland 11).

This American interest in Scotland is mirrored in US romance
fiction:

> Since the early 1990s there has been a rapid growth in mass
> market romance novels that have Scottish settings [...] many
> [...] penned by women, some of whom describe ancestral
> ties to Scotland on cover biographies and websites. (Hague,
> "Mass" 171)

While "these novels are not written with a solely diaspora audience
in mind, its members comprise both authors and readers" (Hague,
"Mass" 190). A plotline representative of those to be found in such
romances is embedded in Joan Hohl's *A Memorable Man* (1997),
in which the hero and heroine gain insight into their roots through
the rather unconventional method of seeing past lives in "scenes that
without warning flashed through my mind" (53). The third such life
recalled by the heroine for her still-sceptical hero is an "incarnation
[which] took place in Scotland" (113):

> "You were what was referred to as a border lord." [...]
> "And you were ...?" he asked [...].
> "The beloved daughter of a peer of the British realm," she
> answered, unsurprisingly.
> What else? Adam reflected, idly wondering what the title
> might be of the historical bodice ripper she had obviously
> been reading prior to those memory flashes.
> "You kidnapped me and held me for ransom."
> Of course. The plot was formulaic, wasn't it? Scotland.
> Border lord. A British peer with a daughter—preferably beau-
> tiful and fiery. A kidnapping. All the elements necessary for a
> satisfying read. Save one.
> "And we fell in love," he said, voicing the last, most impor-
> tant fictional element. (114–15)

By marrying his "beautiful and fiery" captive, Hohl's Scottish "border
lord" "checkmated" (124) the "enemy English" (125).

If Scottish-American identity is flourishing it would appear to
be due in large part to the fact that it, like many other White ethnic
identities, has come to be associated with a history of oppression by
a more powerful White group.

It is a central premise in today's heritage lore that the majority of colonial Scottish immigrants fled their homeland as political refugees after Culloden [...]. Scottish American beliefs that post-Culloden hardships resulted in ancestral immigration inculcate a certain sense of loss and injury—both for the transgenerational loss of a cultural heritage and homeland, and through a revived sense of indignity over ancestral sufferings. (Ray 31)

While Hohl makes no mention of this period, her hero's medieval Scottish incarnation has an English enemy and her heroine's earliest memories are of romantic "tragedy" (52) set against a background of military defeat: the lovers' first incarnation took place in "Britannia [...] during the first century, when the Roman legions conquered the Celtic tribes" (51). While Hohl does not describe these ancient Celts as Scots:

since the eighteenth century, processes of cultural, political and symbolic appropriation have generated powerful and enduringly popular accounts that assume that an ancient Celtic civilisation existed in Scotland and that modern Scotland and its inhabitants are inheritors of this past. [...] In this construction, 'Celticness' and 'Scottishness' often merge, enabling characteristics associated with Scottish and Celtic identities to become interchangeable. (Hague, "The Scottish" 142)

Thus Scottish-Americans, when asked "what Scotland actually means to them" (Sim 146), may refer "not just to Scotland but to a 'Celtic' heritage" (148).

Hohl's protagonists' discussion of their "ancient Celtic heritage" (60) therefore has implications for those Americans who claim a similarly Celtic Scottish heritage by more conventional routes. Discussing their first incarnation the heroine informs her hero that:

"You were the strongest, most fearless warrior in our small tribe. [...] From the little I understood, the tribes consisted of families with a common ancestor. Most of the tribes lived in small rural settlements and raised crops and livestock."

"Not unlike the Native Americans," he mused aloud.

"Yes." Her eyes lit up. "In fact, now that you mention it, there was a similarity." (60)

Comparisons between Celts and Native Americans were also made by the "'Wise Use' movement in Catron County, New Mexico" (McCarthy and Hague 387) which argued for locals' right to greater access to, and use of, federal land:

> Jim Catron […] listed similarities between Native American and Celtic cultures in his [newspaper] columns, describing both as individualistic, democratic warrior cultures, closely tied to the land and resistant to centralization (November 2, 1995, July 11, 1996, July 18, 1996). (404)

In this context, however, there were obvious political implications to the comparisons because "Wise Use's strongest claims to federal lands boiled down to the argument that […] their ancestors had homesteaded the West" (400) and "A major problem with this argument, of course, was that Native American and Hispanic groups, pushed out by the homesteading ancestors of Wise Users […] could advance far stronger historical claims" (401). By drawing parallels between their ancestors and Native Americans, however, Wise Users could position themselves as "*fellow victims* […]. Catron […] and other Wise Use activists emphasized this analogy repeatedly, referring to themselves as 'the new Native Americans' and comparing the Highland clearances to the Trail of Tears" (401).

When an individual's or group's claim to the land is felt by some to be strengthened by merely resembling Native Americans it is hardly surprising that the actual possession of Native American ancestors can cause an American like Nicholas Leclerc, in Joan Domning's *The Forever Man*, to feel "like my existence in this country is a little more justified than most Americans'" (75), even though, as his heroine, Carla, argues, his "native connection is so watered down, it wouldn't stand up in a glass" (75). His comment suggests that, deep down, many non-Native Americans may:

> Like insecure aliens living in someone else's home, […] know the land belongs to other peoples—to Cherokees, Creeks, Chickasaws, Choctaws, Seminoles, Catawbas, and other […]

Indians—in a way it can never belong to us. (Martin 145)

Certainly throughout the history of the USA "Indianness has, above all, represented identities that are unquestionably American. [...] Indianness offered a deep, authentic, aboriginal Americanness" (Deloria 183).

Sharon Brondos's *Doc Wyoming* (1993) is a novel in which a Native American secondary character plays a key role in conferring legitimacy on one White family's roots. It has, however, been suggested that "romance novels [...] function strongly as *national cultural memory* and that they preserve *national cultural experience*" (Linke 196); the prologue of Brondos's novel facilitates this type of broader reading of an individual romance novel. Its:

> geographic stage was classic Rocky Mountain.
> The drama that was soon to take place there was classic western. (7)

and "classic" in this context implies that the western drama which is about to unfold is typical in setting and kind. Furthermore, the event at which the full story of that drama is revealed draws "People from all walks of life, from Wyoming and beyond" (287), Hal Blane's book about his ancestor has "a publisher interested in taking it to a national audience" (291), and there is also "a film company" (291) interested in translating it to the silver screen. It is therefore clear that this is a story of national importance and interest, which speaks to the concerns of a wide range of US popular culture productions and their consumers; when Hattie Blane presents herself at Dr Dixie Sheldon's surgery with "chest pains" (29) perhaps it is time to diagnose a national malaise.

Hattie's pain is, according to:

> "[...] all the other doctors [...] just in my mind, Dr. Sheldon [...] But I feel terrible and my chest *hurts*."
> "I believe you," Dixie said. "And I don't think you're imagining the pain. But organically, you're healthy. [...] What I'd like to look at is your everyday situation. Maybe there we'll find an answer. (31)

The answer, which emerges in the course of sessions in which Hattie and Dixie "just sit and talk" (32), is that Hattie's pain stems from a conviction that "I come from bad people, Doctor. We're all tainted" (133) and that with "the job Hal has? Why, I think it's just a matter of time before he has to kill, too" (140). On a personal level, this would be troubling if true, not least as her son, Hal, is a small-town sheriff; if he is also read as a symbol of the 'world's policeman' the situation is one which ought to cause every American some heartache about US involvement in conflict zones around the globe.

The US's western expansion certainly involved violence (as discussed in Chapter 3) and the appropriation of other people's land. The story of how Hal's family acquired their land is representative of this wider history:

> "This land belonged to my people at a time long past."
> "Native Americans?" Winnie asked.
> "No. Buccaneer English. The Kedricks. On my mother's side. A bad lot. [...] We took it from the Indians. About a hundred years ago." He made a sound like a laugh, but it was too thin to be real mirth. "And then the U.S. government took it from us." He took off his hat and slapped it gently against his leg as if to dislodge dust. "Only fair, I guess." (65–66)

However, the story which plays out in the present, in the pages of Brondos's novel, focuses almost exclusively on the latter appropriation of the land; it does so in a way which both makes it seem unfair and diverts attention away from the fact that the Kedricks certainly took the land "from the Indians", possibly "from the Arapaho" (69).

It had long been thought that "the U.S. Government" gradually took the land from Robert Kedrick's family in retaliation for him taking a "big gold shipment from the army" (70). The role of Dixie and others is "to help find and redeem the past" (239) and thus, in the course of the novel, it becomes clear that Robert Kedrick, rather than being a "thief and a murderer" (196), was in fact the victim of a "web of death and violence and greed" (214). When the Government acquired his land it "wasn't a legitimate governmental land takeover" because the action succeeded "based on poverty brought on by deliberate retributive measures inflicted on the widow of the alleged outlaw, Robert Kedrick" (253). Kedrick was, in fact:

> a government secret agent. The gang he joined as an undercover fed had been making hits for months. [...] Hal should be proud of his ancestor. Undercover agent for the Treasury Department, no less. (253)

Kedrick's "official contact in Treasury" (263), however, "hired Kedrick, figuring to take the gold from him after he and the gang stole it from the army. Kedrick's one big mistake was in trusting a government man" (264).

The narrative thus works to "redeem" the Kedricks, absolving them of guilt by shifting the role of villain onto a source within "the metropolitan regime of authoritarian politics and class privilege" (Slotkin 11):

> [the] entire family has been given a raw deal for almost a century by the government. Or at least some aspect of the government. I don't think the whole U.S. system is to blame, but certainly someone needs to own up to responsibility. (Brondos 217–18)

With Robert Kedrick recast as a victim, he is transformed from one of "a long string of rogues, rounders, roughriders and general bad guys" (80) into an ancestor who can take Hal's place as "the first of my kind to take the side of the law" (80), "the side of the angels" (81):

> he took the job because a close friend had been murdered by that same band of outlaws. Robert figured the best way to get revenge was to get them arrested, tried, and executed for the crime. [...] He wanted revenge, but he was doing it all through legal channels. [...] He never stepped outside the law. (289)

Moreover, as a victim of crime, it is he and his descendants who are acknowledged as deserving of reparation. The solving of the mystery surrounding the stolen gold thus cleanses the family roots.

Any remaining guilt about the role of Whites in taking the land "from the Indians" is removed by Esther, a secondary character who is "at least a hundred years old" (181) and met Robert when she:

"[…] was just a little thing. A baby, really. When he came up here and told my Pa we could stay on his land. […] He was a man who took what he wanted, but he was generous to those who didn't have so much."

"Like your folks?"

"Yes. Not everyone was good to us because my ma was Shoshone." (230)

This neatly glosses over the methods Robert used to acquire the land while portraying him as someone who helped Native Americans and was lacking in the prejudices against them which were held by others.

Esther has further gifts to impart as a result of being:

part Shoshone. […] Well, my ma was full-blood. And she taught me most of what I know and do. I have both white and Indian blood. So, I use both worlds in my healing. (96)

She is a "medicine woman who [has] performed minor miracles out of her kitchen with herbs and incantations" (87) and has "lived in harmony with the wild, raw land and its healthful bounty" (92). As such, she can provide information about "the tips of this plant, […] roots of that, seeds of the other" (180) to Dixie, who eagerly absorbs "all the information the old woman could give her" (181), to share with "a medical center in California that specializes in investigating and utilizing natural and folk medicine under modern scientific techniques and methods" (63).

One might therefore say that Dixie is literally being given Esther's Native American roots. In addition, with her dying breath, Esther addresses Dixie and says:

"Make me a grandmother of your people, child […]. To you, I gave life by killing the one who would have killed you. And I gave you what I know. Now, I give you my spirit. You'll see me in the eyes of your children and their children ..."

And Esther breathed a long sigh, and died. (282)

Dixie has thus spiritually, as well as literally, acquired Native American roots, which she can then share with Hal when they marry. With the family's roots purged of all guilt and embedded deeper in American soil thanks to Esther's gifts, there is no further need of therapy sessions for Hattie. US readers, however, continue to seek out popular fiction, which can be considered a form of collective national therapy because:

> Popular narratives play a vital role in mediating social change, informing their audience of new currents and allowing the reader to insert him- or herself into new scenarios in a way that can be related to her or his own experience. (McCracken 185)

Perhaps the US will require not just the "long-term commitment to therapy—months, maybe years" (Brondos 35) which Dixie foresaw for Hattie, but an almost unlimited number of further sessions before it can fully come to terms with its roots.

Conclusion

Romance publishers largely continue to follow the policy established by the British romance publisher Mills & Boon (which was later absorbed by Harlequin), namely "to avoid 'red-rag' controversial problems—two of which traditionally are politics and religion" (Alan Boon qtd. in McAleer, 190). Indeed, some in the romance publishing community would argue that this seemingly apolitical stance should be extended to authors' non-fictional communications with readers. An article published in the March 2015 issue of the Romance Writers of America's *Romance Writers Report* advised that:

> There are a million polarizing topics. Let's name some: religion. Gay marriage. The ruling in Ferguson, Missouri. Politics. Yes, an author's social media account should tell others who you are, but you are also in the business of selling books.
>
> Leading a somewhat-public life means that while you may have your opinions, you cannot afford to let those opinions turn your readership away. Therefore, should a polarizing issue arise, take a more neutral approach, express sadness or appreciation that the topic is being publically addressed. (Fusco 42)

This advice clearly assumes that the romance authors reading the article do not already explicitly address "polarizing issues" in their fiction; many do, not least the authors of LGBT romances, whose works can very clearly be read as statements in favour of "Gay marriage". Explicit references to religion are essential in 'inspirational' evangelical Christian romances and Lynn S. Neal has observed of historical inspirationals that "The novels' portrayals of the past provide readers with a history where God's control remains constant, evangelicals emerge triumphant, and America is Christian" (178). In the US, "Black women's historical romances document race as a social and political construct" (Dandridge 5).

US interracial romances "written by black women" and featuring "black heroines who are reluctant to enter into a relationship with the white hero" (Blanding 1), depict White men loving and marrying Black women. This challenges racial prejudices because, as Callie, the Black heroine of Roslyn Hardy Holcomb's *Rock Star* (2006) explains to Bryan, the White hero:

> white men have always had a much higher social position than black women in this country. Black women certainly aren't the beauty standard. Most folks see us as either sex objects or baby-making welfare queens. If a white man is with us, it has to be for easy sex. (46–7)

The assumption has always been, however, that interracial romances of this kind, along with lesbian, 'inspirational' and African-American romances, by their very nature attract a relatively niche readership.

So-called "polarizing issues" are, nonetheless, sometimes raised in romances aimed at a wider readership. Suzanne Brockmann's *Harvard's Education* (1998), for instance, was published in Harlequin's Silhouette Intimate Moments line and although it was written long before "The ruling in Ferguson, Missouri" it addresses the issue at the heart of that ruling. The novel's hero, Daryl Becker, recounts how, freshly graduated from Harvard University, he visited New York City and, returning late at night from a jazz concert, decided that:

> it's only a few miles. I'll run. [...] You guessed it. I haven't gone more than four blocks before a police car pulls up alongside me, starts pacing me. Seems that the sight of a black man running in that part of town is enough to warrant a closer look. [...] They get out of the squad car, and it's clear that they don't believe a single word I'm saying, and I'm starting to get annoyed. [...] And I'm telling them that the only reason they even stopped their car was because I'm an African American man [...] and as I'm talking, I'm reaching into my back pocket for my wallet, intending to show these skeptical SOBs my Harvard University ID card, and all of a sudden, I'm looking down the barrel of not one, but two very large police-issue

handguns. (*Harvard's* 147)

This type of incident has been replicated by researchers investigating:

> police officers' decisions to shoot Black and White criminal suspects in a computer simulation. Examination of the officers' responses revealed that, as in previous work using undergraduate samples [...], the officers were initially more likely to mistakenly shoot unarmed Black suspects than unarmed White suspects. (Plant and Peruche 182)

Daryl was lucky, inasmuch as he was not shot and killed by the officers who stopped him. Nonetheless, it was a traumatic experience which convinced him that, as "a six-foot-five black man [...], I'm at risk just walking around" (Brockmann, *Harvard's* 148).

Brockmann recounts that, after the novel's publication, she received "hate-mail" but it also "sold out close to immediately upon publication" and when it "was finally reissued in 2004, it became one of my bestselling categories" ("Embracing"). Clearly Brockmann's political stance did not lose her a significant number of readers but her success in reaching a wide audience while tackling this issue would not necessarily be replicable by other authors. The book was part of a successful series about Navy SEALS; it is possible that because Brockmann was a White author of a series to which they were committed, readers were more inclined to accept her depiction of Daryl and his experiences than they would have been had he appeared in a stand-alone African-American romance. In addition, any anxieties about the US which were elicited by the topic were perhaps mitigated by the hero's profession. In US romances whose protagonists are in the armed services, the "warrior hero has been tied to the rhetoric of democracy and patriotism to varying extents" (Kamble 154).

This is made particularly clear in Brockmann's *Get Lucky* (2000), in which the hero, Lucky O'Donlon, is a Navy SEAL who reveals that his step-father, a refugee:

> reminded me that I lived in a land of freedom [...]. He used to tell me that he could go to sleep at night and be certain that

> no one would break into our house and tear us from our beds. No one would drag us into the street and put bullets in our heads simply for something we believed in. Because of him, I learned to value the freedom that most Americans take for granted. (157)

The novel was published in 2000; on 11 September 2001 America stopped taking freedom from fear for granted "and night fell on a different world, a world where freedom itself is under attack" (Bush). As President George W. Bush told Congress nine days after the attack on the Twin Towers:

> Tonight we are a country awakened to danger and called to defend freedom. Our grief has turned to anger, and anger to resolution. Whether we bring our enemies to justice, or bring justice to our enemies, justice will be done.

Having awakened to the threat to its freedoms, the US would more consciously project its military might outwards. On an individual level Brockmann's Lucky responded in much the same way: he "joined the Navy—the SEAL teams in particular—because [...] I wanted to be a part of making sure we remained the land of the free and the home of the brave" (158).

Bush elaborated on the nature of American freedom by contrasting the US with other nations:

> They hate what we see right here in this chamber—a demo-cratically elected government. Their leaders are self-appoint-ed. They hate our freedoms—our freedom of religion, our freedom of speech, our freedom to vote and assemble and disagree with each other.

He may have been partially correct, but he seemed to ignore the possibility that, sometimes, the US might be hated for denying others "what we see right here in this chamber". Similarly, Lucky's narrative paints the US as a land of freedom and contrasts it with the states in "Central America" which "people were leaving [...] in droves" (155) in the 1970s. Lucky's step-father:

> would tell about these horrible human rights violations he'd

witnessed in his home country. […] "He told me to value my
freedom as an American above all else. [...]" (157)

Although Lucky does admit that "there's a lot wrong with this
country," he quickly adds that "there's also a lot right" (158) and in
his narrative the US's involvement in the lives of Central American
refugees is depicted as wholly benign: it provides refuge to those
who have "managed to escape" (155) from oppression.

This portrayal of the relationship between the US and its 'backyard'
may, however, seem a little odd when one considers the:

> clear and persistent pattern of U.S. influence over the political
> violence conducted by Latin American states. In some cases,
> Latin American governments enthusiastically received U.S.
> support for their campaigns of terror, and in other cases U.S.
> state agencies pressured "weaker" states to undertake such
> campaigns. (Menjívar and Rodríguez, "State" 4–5)

While it is possible that Brockmann was unaware of US support for,
and encouragement of, governments which "would drag us into the
street and put bullets in our heads simply for something we believed
in", it was in 1994, long before the publication of Brockmann's novel,
that the US mainstream media began to offer:

> a clear presentation of the links between the United States and
> Guatemalan right-wing violence […], in this […] coverage a
> clear and consistent link was made between long-term U.S.
> policies and Guatemalan security forces and death squads.
> (Livingston and Eachus 431)

The revelations demonstrated that the U.S. supported repressive
governments in this Central American state during the period to
which Lucky alludes:

> In an April 2, 1995, article, the *Washington Post*'s R. Jeffery
> Smith and Dana Priest outlined the assistance and training
> provided by the United States to a succession of Guatemalan
> military governments between 1962 and 1976. (Livingston
> and Eachus 432)

In March 1999, while on a tour of Central America, President Clinton:

> admitted that the United States provided support for wide-spread repression in Guatemala's thirty-six-year reign of military and paramilitary terror. (Menjívar and Rodríguez, "New" 344)

and:

> He also promised "to do everything I possibly can" to eliminate discriminatory provisions in U.S. immigration laws that favor refugees from Cuba and Nicaragua over those who fled to the United States to escape right-wing governments in Guatemala and El Salvador that were supported by Washington. (Gerstenzang and Darling)

None of this, however, would appear to have dented the belief held by Lucky and countless other other Americans that the US is a state unambiguously synonymous with freedom.

Shaping the nation's self-image is the persistent conviction that:

> Providence, or history, has put a special responsibility on the American people to spread the blessings of liberty, democracy, and equality to others throughout the earth, and to defeat, if necessary by force, the sinister powers of darkness. (Tuveson viii)

Bush gave expression to this belief when he declared that:

> in our grief and anger we have found our mission and our moment. Freedom and fear are at war. The advance of human freedom—the great achievement of our time, and the great hope of every time—now depends on us. Our nation—this generation—will lift a dark threat of violence from our people and our future. We will rally the world to this cause by our efforts, by our courage.

Though the mission was a new one, the cause itself was not, for "We have seen their kind before. They are the heirs of all the murderous ideologies of the 20th century [...]—they follow in the path of fascism, and Nazism, and totalitarianism" (Bush). By presenting the "war on terror" as a continuation of the Second World War and the Cold War, Bush was able to emphasise both the geographical and chronological scope of the struggle ahead and, through his allusion to the evils of "fascism, and Nazism, and totalitarianism", he clearly positioned the US in opposition to "the sinister powers of darkness" (Tuveson viii).

LaVyrle Spencer

Brockmann's *Get Lucky* makes explicit a widely held, and deeply political, belief about the US but the fact is that no romance can be completely apolitical. As author Courtney Milan has admitted:

> truthfully, no matter how little a writer says about politics, her books inevitably betray at least some of the things that are nearest and dearest to her heart. [...] It's never intended as a lecture, but when an author chooses a "happily ever after," the *way* she makes her characters happy often shows what she thinks people need.

LaVyrle Spencer, for example, was an author who, when asked about her success, felt:

> comfortable telling them that I was a success before I got published, for I'd accomplished the far more important goal of creating a marriage and a home filled with love, and raising two neat children. (Falk 268)

In *Morning Glory* (1989) "the *way* she makes her characters happy" strongly suggests that "she thinks people need" "a marriage and a home filled with love, and [...] children" in order to be happy. An analysis of *Morning Glory* demonstrates that this is not a wholly apolitical belief.

The novel is set in August of 1941, and thus shortly before the US entered the fight against "the murderous ideologies of the 20th century" (Bush). Spencer herself was born in 1943 and in the years which followed:

> Heterosexual Americans [...] became emblematic of what it meant to be an American. The American home, populated by a heterosexual couple and their children, became, symbolically

and literally, a fortress against the anxieties provoked by the Cold War. (Lewis 4)

The novel's historical setting, in conjunction with the context in which its author grew to adulthood, perhaps facilitated the creation of a romance which, like the nineteenth-century "foundational fictions" of Latin America, "collapses the distinctions" between "nationalism and intimate sensibility" (Sommer 24). As with the nineteenth-century US "cult of domesticity", the "*domestic* has a double meaning that not only links the familial household to the nation but also imagines both in opposition to everything outside the geographic and conceptual border of the home" (Kaplan 581).

This is extremely apparent in the depiction of two secondary characters: Lydia Marsh and Lula Peak. When the former takes the stand at the trial to determine who murdered the latter, she appeals to "the sense of patriotism running rife through every American in that jurors' box" (Spencer, *Morning* 367–8) because she is as "pretty as a madonna" and is "a housewife and mother of two whose husband was fighting 'somewhere in Italy.'" (367). She looks "sweet, not hard like Lula Peak" (255), who is portrayed as a self-centred, materialistic, amoral woman whose attitude towards children is a factor in her murder. At the time of her death, Lula was using her pregnancy as a tool to blackmail her married lover, Harley Overmire, and when she had the gall to approach his underage son and then point out to the former that the:

> boy [...] is gettin' better lookin' by the day. [...]
> The threat was clear [...] and it was the last straw. When she started in on the kids, it was time to put a stop to Lula Peak. (325)

Although the law seeks to identify her murderer, no-one truly regrets Lula's death and the reader's sympathy is directed instead towards Will, the hero, who is wrongfully accused of the crime because some years before he had inadvertently killed Honey Rossiter after hitting her with a bottle because "If I hadn't clunked her, she'd have shot Josh smack through his left eye" (163).

The similarities between Lula and Honey are not limited to the violent manner of their deaths or the fact that Honey was a prostitute while Lula is described as a "whore" (89) and a "harlot" (90). Lula can be said to have perverted motherhood by using her pregnancy as a bargaining chip and threatening to abuse her future stepson; Honey rejected it, declaring that "she'd have to be crazy to marry a no-count saddle bum who'd probably keep her pregnant nine months out of twelve and expect her to take care of a houseful of his squallin' brats" (162). Honey's duplicitous ability to appear to be "whatever a man needed" (162) destroyed the small community created by Will and his friend Josh because when the matter came to trial Josh:

> Told this sob story about how he was gonna make an honest woman out of Honey Rossiter [...] and give her a home and respectability. And the jury fell for it. I did five years for savin' my *friend's* life. (163)

Lula threatened the stability of her lover's family and her death puts Will's in jeopardy.

Lula's murder, however, occurred during wartime, when men were being drafted to fight for their country and their efforts were supported by rationing on the "home front". In this context the domestic is inescapably political and the stakes are therefore raised, even if only symbolically, when a family is under attack: when war-hero Will is framed by Harley, who has "a countywide reputation as a military shirker" (381), and incarcerated, the liberty of the nation as a whole seems at risk. Moreover, when motherhood forms an essential part of an American ideal which evokes "a sense of patriotism", women who sully or reject it can perhaps be considered a dangerous fifth column that threatens to destroy the nation from within. It seems no coincidence that Lula's main concern during the war was for her own comfort: "It deprived her of everything she cared most about: nylon stockings, chocolate ice cream—and men" (317), and she therefore railed against "That damn Roosevelt [who] had control of everything—no cars, no bobby pins, no hair dryers" (317) and was "riled [...] by having to do without nylons. How the hell many parachutes did they need anyway?" (317).

While *Morning Glory* only implies a correlation between a lack of patriotism and a self-centred willingness to engage in acts that endanger family life, it explicitly links love for one's family with a willingness to take up arms in their defence. Will, on hearing the declaration of war following the attack on Pearl Harbour:

> was surprised to find himself fired with some of the same outrage as that conflagrating through the rest of America: for the first time Will felt the righteousness of President Roosevelt's "Four Freedoms" because for the first time he enjoyed them all. And being a family man made them the more dear. (230–1)

The "Four Freedoms" were: "freedom of speech and expression"; "freedom of every person to worship God in his own way"; "freedom from want"; "freedom from fear" (Roosevelt 20–1). At the beginning of the novel the first was alien to Will who:

> wasn't used to being allowed to speak his mind. Prison had taught him the road to the least troubles was to keep his mouth shut. It felt strange, being granted the freedom to say what he would. (Spencer, *Morning* 21)

Alone and hungry he "shut out the pain and transported himself to a place he'd never seen, where smiles were plentiful, and plates full, and people nice to one another" (7). He finds it in Elly's home and here, too, he experiences freedom from fear. As she puts her sons to bed:

> Will watched Eleanor kiss them goodnight, smiling at the scene. Two pajama-clad boys with faces scrubbed shiny being reassured by their mother that they were loved [...]. With a pang of awe he realized he would be part of this tableau every night. (152)

With only slight alterations in the particulars, this tableau, and that of the "place he'd never seen", can be found among Norman Rockwell's famous paintings of the Freedoms. Like Will, Rockwell seems to have felt that the Freedoms were best understood in the context of the family and so "in two of the four paintings, the message was that the people of the United States were fighting for the family" (Westbrook 203). In *Freedom from Fear* "Rockwell [...] depicted parents tucking in their sleeping children" (Murray and McCabe 20) while:

> *Freedom from Want* probably aroused in Americans their warmest, happiest memories. Who could forget that huge turkey in the center of the picture, the benign older couple still serving as nurturing grandparents, the excited, happy faces of young and old around the table? (James McGregor Burns qtd. in Murray and McCabe, 104)

At the outbreak of war in 1941 Will could not have seen these paintings since they were not completed until 1943 but they may have influenced Spencer, who was an admirer of Rockwell's: in 1996, just seven years after *Morning Glory* was published, she and her husband "toured the Norman Rockwell Museum in Stockbridge, Massachusetts for the second time (We love it!)" (*Small Town* 379).

Rockwell is not mentioned by name in *Forsaking All Others* (1982) but this is a romance which opens "With sly self-referentiality" (Maynard) as Allison Scott, the novel's photographer heroine, is trying to locate models for the cover of a romance; its penultimate chapter shows her attending "a workshop and symposium down at University of Wisconsin called Photographing People for Profit" (Spencer, *Forsaking* 218). One may, therefore, be justified in reading the novel as, in part, a commentary on commercial art. Allison succeeds in selling some photographs she took at a Winterfest, where she captured on camera:

> two runny-nosed eight-year-olds angling for sunfish through a hole in the ice; the laughing face of a man who'd fallen onto his back like an overturned turtle during a game of broomball; [...] a string of red-nosed youngsters at the finish line of an ice-skating race, their lips set in grim determination; a boy and girl kissing, unaware that Allison was snapping them because their eyes were closed. (167)

These, surely, are scenes which would have appealed to Rockwell, who "wrote in 1936 [...] 'Boys batting flies on vacant lots; little girls playing jacks on the front steps; old men plodding home at twilight, umbrellas in hand—all of these things arouse feeling in me. [...]'" (Moffatt 24). Although Allison has "an artist's soul, an enviable talent behind the viewfinder" (Spencer, *Forsaking* 45), Rick, the hero of *Forsaking All Others*, acknowledges that these photographs depict "stuff that to some would seem so ridiculously bourgeois they'd scoff at the suggestion of even coming here, much less recording the homey events on film" (168). Such people would presumably feel similarly about the work of Norman Rockwell, who has been described as:

> the American painter most typically regarded as the virtuoso of the ordinary [...] whose illustrations provide a rich assortment of artifacts often implicated in the taste of kitsch and the banal elevation of the quotidian to a level of cultural importance. (Binkley 143)

Rockwell himself, while acknowledging that he painted "ordinary people in everyday situations" (349), argued that he could "fit most anything into that frame, even fairly big ideas" (349). LaVyrle Spencer's *Morning Glory* seems to do much the same: it uses the romantic frame of a love story to present the reader with a vision of an ideal America.

The US has often been conceived of as a woman:

> At the opening of each new territory, in fact, the maternal and the sexual were invoked together; in Wisconsin it was said, 'the land foams with creamy milk, and the hollow trees trickle with wild honey.' (Kolodny 67)

Similarly, although Elly, the heroine of *Morning Glory*, becomes Will's "wife, not his mother, yet he loved her as if she were both" (Spencer, *Morning* 237): she is "the mother/wife he would always need her to be" (315). She too flows with milk and honey although, appropriately for a symbol of the US in a novel which opens as America is "Just emerging from the jaws of the depression" (29), when she first appears in the text she is "barefoot, her skirt faded, its hem sagging to the right, her blouse the color of muddy water, her entire appearance as shabby as her place" (12). There are, nonetheless, hints of her abundance and that of the land with which she is closely identified: Elly's fecundity is incontestable given that she already has two children and is "pregnant as hell" (13) with a third. It will, then, be only months until she, like her cow which "gives more than we can use" (53), will flow with milk. She cannot, of course, literally flow with honey but her "unkempt" hair is "honey-brown, and he wondered if with a washing it might not turn honeyer" (20). It does, just as the "hives he'd at first believed abandoned by the insects" (103) are found to be "laden with honey" (104). Honey has particular symbolic resonance in the context of American history:

> From the earliest days of colonization, white Christians had represented their journey across the Atlantic to America as the exodus of a New Israel from the bondage of Egypt into the Promised Land of milk and honey. (Raboteau 81)

In promising her land and herself in marriage to a "healthy man of any age willing to work a spread and share the place" (Spencer, *Morning* 10), Elly and her spread can be read as a representation of the promised land, America itself.

Given this, and the fact that Elly's "white house" (389) is located on a "hill" (14), at the top of a "steep, rocky" (12) road, it can perhaps be considered a homely microcosm of the "shining city upon a hill". Spencer wrote *Morning Glory* during the presidency of Ronald Reagan who:

> Throughout his political life [...] spoke of his vision for America as a shining city on a hill—an image he borrowed from John Winthrop (1588–1649), the godly Puritan who served as the first governor of the Massachusetts colony. (Reagan 33)

This was a view of the US which would have been held by many US citizens during the period in which *Morning Glory* is set, for although:

> prior to 1945 it was unusual to find Americans endorsing the idea that the United States should be, or had to be, a permanent guardian of international order [...i]n the popular American conception, the United States was a haven for the disadvantaged [...]; was an example to the rest of mankind (the "city upon a hill"); and would, and could, intervene decisively on the side of "good" when disorder in the Old World so required. (Gray 29–30)

When Spencer wrote *Morning Glory*, either towards, or just after, the end of the Reagan presidency, the US had accepted its role as a global super-power and one can detect support for interventionism in the novel itself: Will leaves home to serve his country overseas and when he is accused of murdering Lula, Elly abandons her policy of domestic isolationism in order to ensure justice for him. Only by engaging with the outside world can they prove they're "as good as any of them down there—better […] You got to go down into that town and show 'em" (Spencer, *Morning* 250).

After Will's acquittal, and the ensuing "handshakes" and "smiles" with which their "fellow townspeople" welcome Will "and Elly into their fold at last" (384), Spencer concludes her novel with her protagonists' return to their home on the hill where Elly, pregnant with her fourth child, will once again be flowing with milk and where "the bees would soon make the honey run again" (389). It is an ending which would presumably have pleased George Washington, who once wrote that he wished:

> to see the sons and daughters of the world in peace, and busily employed in the more agreeable amusement of fulfilling the first and great commandment, *increase and multiply*. As an encouragement to it, we have opened the fertile plains […] to the poor, the needy, the oppressed, of the earth; any one, there-fore, who is heavy laden, or who wants land to cultivate, may repair here, and make it overflow, as in the land of promise, with milk and honey. (115)

Given Washington's status as a slave owner and his stipulation that the settlers work and multiply, one may suspect that "the sons and daughters of the world" he had in mind were White, heterosexual, non-disabled and relatively young, just like the protagonists who have been, and indeed continue to be, the norm in US romances.

Admittedly "the number of romances that include multicultural characters seems to be on the rise […] and […] many of these romances are slipping into the mainstream" (Ramsdell 442). In addition, as reported by Canada's *The Globe and Mail* in 2011, there has been a noteworthy increase in romances featuring two male protagonists:

> Over the past year, man-on-man romantic fiction—books fea-

turing two male protagonists engaged in a sexual or emotional relationship with each other—has taken a significant bite out of one of publishing's biggest markets. Amazon's Kindle has had such success with the genre that the e-book site has tripled its "m/m" stock since January, 2010. (Iannacci)

Increased visibility can not, however, automatically be assumed to be an unalloyed good. Even apparently well-intentioned depictions may be problematic. For instance, Hilary Radner argues that in LaVyrle Spencer's *The Hellion* (1984) the heroine's maid, Callie Mae, is a "stereotyped 'mammy'" (101), an African-American figure whose "role is to care for the white women" (101).

In an earlier novel Spencer had broken an unwritten rule of romance publishing in this period: "The woman of color is rarely if ever the heroine" (Radner 101). It nonetheless seems significant that Lee Walker, the heroine of *A Promise to Cherish* (1983), unlike the African-American supporting characters of *The Hellion*, is "One quarter Cherokee" (40): in the mainstream romance fiction of the last quarter of the twentieth century "'Native American' is an acceptable romanticized racial category, where African American is not" (Burley 334). It should also be noted that Lee's experience of racism is questioned and, eventually, dismissed as largely self-inflicted. The hero, Sam, asks Lee if she has "a hang-up about being Indian" (Spencer, *A Promise* 80), observes that she's "very defensive about it" (142), and finally lectures her about her attitude:

> Sam's face was grim. "Lee, you've got a red chip on your shoulder about the size of the original Indian nations! You carry it there, daring anybody to knock it off—that's why most people try. When are you going to learn you're melted into the pot here, and stop flaunting your heritage?" (231)

The "melting pot" is "a political symbol used to strengthen and legitimize the ideology of America as a land of opportunity where race, religion, and national origin should not be barriers to social mobility" (Hirschman 398). On a small scale, Sam's hiring policy epitomises this ideal: his employees are so diverse in terms of age, gender and race that after they have "begun their work day, Lee

[…] felt as if she were in the amphitheater of the United Nations Building!" (Spencer, *A Promise* 98).

The novel as a whole would seem to endorse Sam's view of America as a melting pot because he himself can be taken as proof of the veracity of his assertions. His surname, Brown, is an anglicised version of Brunvedt (44), which suggests that "somewhere back along the line" (44) one of his Norwegian ancestors made an effort to be assimilated into American culture. Sam himself is a successful businessman who has "melted into the pot" so well that although his eyes are "deep brown in a tan face" (10), he can pass for White. On first meeting him, Lee identifies only the "narrow, Nordic" (10) nose he inherited from his "hard-drinking, hard-working Norwegian" (43) father and she remains unaware of "the truth about his heritage" (161) until over half-way through the novel, when she finally discovers his "mother is more Indian than I am" (158). The clear implication of all this, and of Sam's comment concerning the "red chip" on Lee's shoulder, is that if Lee experiences racism it is because she "flaunts" her ethnic origins, for instance via the "ever-present feathers" (32) she wears or her "Indian jewelry" (142).

Similar condemnations of an ethnic minority character who "flaunts" his "heritage" can be found in Spencer's *Family Blessings* (1994) in a scene which, in linguist Rosina Lippi-Green's opinion, "provides a typical social construction of an idealized relationship between an *SAE [Standard American English] speaker and an AAVE [African American Vernacular English] speaker" (193). The speaker of AAVE is Judd Quincy, a "poor little bastard. No question he was one. His mother and 'dad' were white. Judd was pale brown" (Spencer, *Family* 100). He is described as undergoing "an identity crisis. Half the time he talked like a semi-educated white kid, the other half he broke into black rap" (101). Chris, the hero of the novel and a White police officer, befriends Judd, critiques his use of English, and tells him that "if you want to […] make something of yourself […] you start by talking like a smart person" (103): in his opinion, Judd's linguistic choices demonstrate he's "preserving the wrong side of your culture" (103). As Lippi-Green observes:

AAVE seems to symbolize African American resistance to a

cultural mainstreaming process which is seen as the logical and reasonable cost of equality—and following from that, success—in other realms. [...] The reasoning seems to be that the logical conclusion to a successful civil rights movement is the end of racism not because we have come to accept difference, but because we have eliminated difference. There will be no need for a distinct African American [...] culture (or language), because those people will have full access to, and control of, the superior European American one. (194)

Chris's statements, like the anglicisation of Sam's surname and his suggestion that Lee stop "flaunting" her heritage, would seem to indicate that although the "melting pot" metaphor used by Sam and others "suggests a blending of cultures, the process was essentially one of 'anglo-conformity'" (Hirschman 398) which required immigrants to:

learn English, shed their "foreign" culture, and become "American." Tension exists, however, because some immigrants resist complete assimilation. Moreover, racial and other differences prevent full acceptance by dominant society of some minority groups. (K. Johnson 1278)

Slavery and Jim Crow laws, for instance, imposed separation on African-Americans and even today:

a formally race-neutral criminal justice system can manage to round up, arrest, and imprison an extraordinary number of black and brown men, when people of color are actually no more likely to be guilty of drug crimes and many other offenses than whites. [...] In many respects, release from prison does not represent the beginning of freedom but instead [...] discrimination against them in voting, employment, housing, education, public benefits, and jury service. (Alexander 17)

In *The New Jim Crow: Mass Incarceration in the Age of Color-blindness* (2010), Michelle Alexander argues that this situation has arisen because, despite the formal ending of slavery, "the notion of racial difference—specifically the notion of white supremacy—proved far more durable than the institution that gave birth to it"

(26) and so, to this day, the American criminal justice system is deeply influenced by "conscious and unconscious racial beliefs and stereotypes" (103).

LaVyrle Spencer's novels demonstrate that implicitly, and sometimes explicitly, US romance novels express political 'truths' that the majority of Americans have held to be self-evident: that "Family values are the most valuable American values" (Nachbar and Lause 95), that the US is a land of opportunity (particularly for those willing to work hard) and that it has a special responsibility to spread freedom and democracy internationally. There may be, as romance author Emma Barry puts it, "a literary culture that denies the political dimension of most texts [...] pretending that a run-of-the-mill Regency or small-town contemporary is without statement about power or politics" ("Politics") but, as the best-selling Jayne Ann Krentz has stated:

> it's in popular fiction that we preserve our society's, our culture's, core values. You know, people complain they're not taught in school, people complain that nobody goes to church any more, people complain that nobody understands what core values are anymore, but that's baloney. We read them. We know exactly what a hero is supposed to do. We may not do it ourselves but we sure know what the truth is and we learn that not so much from the institutions but from our popular fiction and that's why it survives: we need it. ("Why")

Whether set in the past, the present, an imagined future or a fantasy world, popular romances "attempt to mold the political and social forces that drive and limit our intimate lives into the shape of a wish come true" (Ostrov Weisser 169). On occasion, however, they have been known to suggest that the light of the "shining city upon a hill" is not quite as bright as many would like to believe.

Bibliography

Romance Novels

Banning, Lynna. *Smoke River Bride*. Don Mills, Ontario: Harlequin, 2013.

Barry, Emma. *Party Lines*. n.p: Carina, 2015.

Brockmann, Suzanne. *Get Lucky*. Richmond, Surrey: Silhouette, 2000.

Brockmann, Suzanne. *Harvard's Education*. 1998. Richmond, Surrey: Silhouette, 1999.

Brondos, Sharon. *Doc Wyoming*. Don Mills, Ontario: Harlequin, 1993.

Browning, Pamela. *Feathers in the Wind*. Don Mills, Ontario: Harlequin, 1989.

Burton, Mary. *A Bride for McCain*. 2000. Richmond, Surrey: Harlequin Mills & Boon, 2003.

Dale, Ruth Jean. *Legend!* 1993. Richmond, Surrey: Harlequin Mills & Boon, 1997.

Davis, Justine. *Deadly Temptation*. 2007. Richmond, Surrey: Harlequin Mills & Boon, 2009.

Domning, Joan J. *The Forever Man*. Hicksville, NY: Bantam, 1993.

Hohl, Joan. *A Memorable Man*. New York, NY: Silhouette, 1997.

Holcomb, Roslyn Hardy. *Rock Star*. Columbus, MS: Genesis, 2006.

Jenkins, Beverly. *Belle*. 2002 [First published as *Belle and the Beau*] New York, NY: Kimani, 2009.

Johnston, Joan. *A Wolf in Sheep's Clothing*. 1991. Richmond, Surrey: Silhouette, 1992.

Kallmaker, Karin. *In Every Port*. 1989. Tallahassee, Florida: Naiad, 1998.

Krentz, Jayne Ann. *Trust Me*. London: Mandarin, 1995.

Lackey, Mercedes. *Beauty and the Werewolf*. Don Mills, Ontario: LUNA, 2011.

Langhorne, Karyn. *Street Level: An Urban Fairytale*. New York, New York: HarperTorch, 2005.

Lerner, Rose. *In for a Penny*. New York: Dorchester, 2010.

McCauley, Barbara. *Texas Heat*. Richmond, Surrey: Silhouette, 1995.

McGill, Joyce. *Unforgivable*. New York: New York: Silhouette, 1992.

Morsi, Pamela. *Simple Jess*. New York: Jove, 1996.

Richards, Emilie. *Gilding the Lily*. New York, NY: Silhouette, 1985.

Roberts, Nora. *The Fall of Shane MacKade*. 1996. *The MacKades: Devin & Shane*. Richmond, Surrey: Silhouette, 2008.

Roberts, Nora. *The Heart of Devin MacKade*. 1996. *The MacKades: Devin & Shane*. Richmond, Surrey: Silhouette, 2008.

Roberts, Nora. *The Pride of Jared MacKade*. 1995. *The MacKades: Rafe & Jared*. Richmond, Surrey: Silhouette, 2008.

Roberts, Nora. *The Return of Rafe MacKade*. 1995. *The MacKades: Rafe & Jared*. Richmond, Surrey: Silhouette, 2008.

Schulze, Dallas. *Stormwalker*. 1987. Richmond, Surrey: Harlequin, 1988.

Shinn, Sharon. *Dark Moon Defender*. 2006. New York: Ace, 2007.

Shinn, Sharon. *Fortune and Fate*. 2008. New York: Ace, 2009.

Shinn, Sharon. *Mystic and Rider*. 2005. New York: Ace, 2006.

Shinn, Sharon. *Reader and Raelynx*. 2007. New York: Ace, 2008.

Shinn, Sharon. *The Thirteenth House*. 2006. New York: Ace, 2007.

Shinn, Sharon. "When Winter Comes". *The Queen in Winter*. New York: Berkley, 2006. 83–164.

Sinclair, Linnea. *Games of Command*. New York: Bantam Dell, 2007.

Spencer, LaVyrle. *A Promise to Cherish*. 1983. New York: Jove, 2004.

Spencer, LaVyrle. *Family Blessings*. 1994. London: HarperCollins, 1995.

Spencer, LaVyrle. *Forsaking All Others*. 1982. New York: Jove, 2003.

Spencer, LaVyrle. *Morning Glory*. 1989. New York: Jove, 1990.

Spencer, LaVyrle. *Small Town Girl*. 1997. New York: Jove, 1998.

Stark, Nell. *Homecoming*. New York: Bold Strokes, 2008.

St. John, Cheryl. *Saint or Sinner*. 1995. Richmond, Surrey: Harlequin Mills & Boon, 2004.

Weir, Theresa. *Loving Jenny*. New York, NY: Silhouette, 1989.

Welsh, Kate. *Texan's Honour*. Richmond, Surrey: Mills & Boon, 2012.

Wind, Ruth. *Meant to be Married*. 1998. Richmond, Surrey: Silhouette, 1999.

Wolf, Joan. *Affair of the Heart*. New York: Rapture Romance, 1984.

Other Texts Cited

Alexander, Michelle. *The New Jim Crow: Mass Incarceration in the Age of Colorblindness*. 2010. New York: The New P, 2012.

Allan, Jonathan A. "Theorising Male Virginity in Popular Romance Novels". *Journal of Popular Romance Studies* 2.1 (2011). <http://jprstudies.org/2011/10/theorising-male-virginity/>.

Arneil, Barbara. *Diverse Communities: The Problem with Social Capital*. Cambridge: Cambridge UP, 2006.

Baldys, Emily M. "Disabled Sexuality, Incorporated: The Compulsions of Popular Romance". *Journal of Literary and Cultural Disability Studies* 6.2 (2012): 125–41.

Barry, Emma. "Politics and the Romance Novel". 28 May 2013. <http://authoremmabarry.com/2013/05/28/politics-and-the-romance-novel/>.

Basu, Paul. "Route Metaphors of 'Roots-Tourism' in the Scottish Highland Diaspora". *Reframing Pilgrimage: Cultures in Motion*. Ed. Simon Coleman and John Eade. London: Routledge, 2004. 150–74.

Baum, L. Frank. *The Wizard of Oz*. New York: Scholastic, 1958.

Baym, Nina. "A History of American Women's Western Books, 1833–1928". *A Companion to the Literature and Culture of the American West.* Ed. Nicolas S. Witschi. Blackwell Companions to Literature and Culture 74. Chichester, West Sussex: Wiley-Blackwell, 2011. 63–80.

Bederman, Gail. *Manhood & Civilization: A Cultural History of Gender and Race in the United States, 1880–1917.* 1995. Chicago: U of Chicago P, 1996.

Bernstein, Paul. *American Work Values: Their Origin and Development.* Albany, NY: State U of New York P, 1997.

Bettinotti, Julia. "Re-imagining the Gold Rush: Prospectors, Log Cabins and Mail-Order Brides in Contemporary Western Romances". *Northern Review* 19 (1998): 170–80.

Betz, Phyllis M. *Lesbian Romance Novels: A History and Critical Analysis.* Jefferson, North Carolina: McFarland, 2009.

Binkley, Sam. "Kitsch as a Repetitive System: A Problem for the Theory of Taste Hierarchy". *Journal of Material Culture* 5.2 (2000): 131–52.

Bird, S. Elizabeth. "Gendered Construction of the American Indian in Popular Media". *Journal of Communication* 49.3 (1999): 61–83.

Blanding, Cristen. *Interracial Romance Novels and the Resolution of Racial Difference.* MA Thesis, Bowling Green State University, 2005. <https://etd.ohiolink.edu/!etd.send_file?accession=bgsu1131365873&disposition=inline>.

Bloomberg BusinessWeek. "Romance Fiction: Getting Dirty in Dutch County". 22 July 2010. <http://www.businessweek.com/magazine/content/10_31/b4189069953563.htm>.

Bowring, Michèle A. "Resistance Is *Not* Futile: Liberating Captain Janeway from the Masculine-Feminine Dualism of Leadership". *Gender, Work and Organization* 11.4 (2004): 381–405.

Braddock, David L. and Susan L. Parish. "An Institutional History of Disability". *Handbook of Disability Studies.* Ed. Gary L. Albrecht, Katherine D. Seelman and Michael Bury. Thousand Oaks, California: Sage, 2001. 11–68.

Broadway, Chuck. "Fourth FW Holds Historic Change of Command". Seymour Johnson Air Force Base. 1 June 2012. <http://www.seymourjohnson.af.mil/news/story.asp?id=123304401>.

Brockmann, Suzanne. "Embracing the 'Other'". *Celebrate Romance*. 26 August 2013. <http://www.readaromancemonth.com/2013/08/day-26-suzanne-brockmann-embracing-the-other/>.

Brown, Hilary. "'An Ordinary Sexual Life?': A Review of the Normalisation Principle as it Applies to the Sexual Options of People with Learning Disabilities". *Disability & Society* 9.2 (1994): 123–44.

Browne, Ray B. "Popular Culture as the New Humanities". *Journal of Popular Culture* 17.4 (1984): 1–8.

Burley, Stephanie. "Shadows & Silhouettes: The Racial Politics of Category Romance". *Paradoxa* 5.13–14 (2000): 324–43.

Bush, George W. "Address to a Joint Session of Congress and the American People". *The White House*. 20 Sept. 2001. <http://georgewbush-whitehouse.archives.gov/news/releases/2001/09/20010920-8.html>.

Byrom, Brad. "A Pupil and a Patient: Hospital-Schools in Progressive America". *The New Disability History: American Perspectives*. Ed. Paul K. Longmore and Lauri Umansky. New York: New York UP, 2001. 133–56.

Carroll, Lewis. *Through the Looking-Glass*. 1871. *Alice's Adventures in Wonderland* and *Through the Looking-Glass and What Alice Found There*. Ed. Roger Lancelyn Green. Oxford: Oxford UP, 1998. 113–245.

Cawelti, John G. *The Six-Gun Mystique Sequel*. Bowling Green, OH: Bowling Green State U Popular P, 1999.

Celello, Kristin. *Making Marriage Work: A History of Marriage and Divorce in the Twentieth-Century United States*. Chapel Hill: U of North Carolina P, 2009.

Chappel, Deborah K. "LaVyrle Spencer and the Anti-Essentialist Argument". *Paradoxa* 3.1-2 (1997): 107–20.

Chesser, Eustace. *How to Make a Success of Your Marriage*. 1952.

London: May Fair, 1962.

Chevalier, Michel. *Society, Manners and Politics in the United States: Being a Series of Letters on North America*. Trans. T. G. Bradford. Boston: Weeks, Jordan, 1839. <http://archive.org/details/societymanners00chev>.

Clarke, Kamari Maxine. "Mapping Transnationality: Roots Tourism and the Institutionalization of Ethnic Heritage". *MacMillan Center for African Studies* 9 (2005): 73–96. <http://www.isn.ethz.ch/Digital-Library/Publications/Detail/?ots591=0c54e3b3-1e9c-be1e-2c24-a6a8c7060233&lng=en&id=47054>.

Clawson, Laura. "Cowboys and Schoolteachers: Gender in Romance Novels, Secular and Christian". *Sociological Perspectives* 48.4 (2005): 461–79.

Cohn, D'Vera and Rich Morin. *American Mobility: Who Moves? Who Stays Put? Where's Home?* Pew Research Center, 2008. <http://www.pewsocialtrends.org/files/2011/04/American-Mobility-Report-updated-12-29-08.pdf>.

Cohn, Jan. *Romance and the Erotics of Property: Mass-Market Fiction for Women*. Durham, NC: Duke UP, 1988.

Commons, John R. and John B. Andrews. *A Documentary History of American Industrial Society Vol. X: Labor Movement, 1860–1880, Volume 2*. Cleveland, OH: Arthur H. Clark, 1911. <http://archive.org/details/documentaryhisto10commuoft>.

Cook, Nancy. "Home on the Range: Montana Romances and Geographies of Hope". *All Our Stories Are Here: Critical Perspectives on Montana Literature*. Ed. Brady Harrison. Lincoln, NE: U of Nebraska P, 2009. 55–77.

Cranny-Francis, Anne. "Sexuality and Role-Stereotyping in *Star Trek*". *Science Fiction Studies* 12 (1985): 274–84.

Creamer, Deborah Beth. *Disability and Christian Theology: Embodied Limits and Constructive Possibilities*. New York: Oxford UP, 2009.

Crothers, Lane. *Globalization and American Popular Culture: Third Edition*. Lanham, Maryland: Rowman & Littlefield, 2013.

Crusie, Jennifer. "Picture This: Collage as Prewriting and Inspiration". First published in *Romance Writer's Report*. Feb. 2003. <http://www.jennycrusie.com/for-writers/essays/picture-this-collage-as-prewriting-and-inspiration/>.

Dandridge, Rita B. *Black Women's Activism: Reading African American Women's Historical Romances*. New York: Peter Lang, 2004.

DeGroot, Gerard J. "A Few Good Women: Gender Stereotypes, the Military and Peacekeeping". *International Peacekeeping* 8.2 (2001): 23–38.

Deloria, Philip J. *Playing Indian*. New Haven: Yale UP, 1998.

Diamond, Larry. *The Spirit of Democracy: The Struggle to Build Free Societies Throughout the World*. New York: Holt, 2008.

Donadio, Rachel. "Promotional Intelligence". *New York Times*. 21 May 2006. <http://www.nytimes.com/2006/05/21/books/review/21donadio.html>.

Doosje, Bertjan E. J, Nyla R. Branscombe, Russell Spears and Antony S. R. Manstead. "Antecedents and Consequences of Group-Based Guilt: The Effects of Ingroup Identification". *Group Processes & Intergroup Relations* 9.3 (2006): 325–38.

Durnbaugh, Donald F. "Communitarian Societies in Colonial America". *America's Communal Utopias*. Ed. Donald E. Pitzer. Chapel Hill, NC: U of North Carolina P, 1997. 14–36.

Ehnenn, Jill. "Desperately Seeking Susan Among the Trash: Reinscription, Subversion and Visibility in the Lesbian Romance Novel". *Atlantis* 23.1 (1998): 120–7.

Falk, Kathryn. "LaVyrle Spencer". *Love's Leading Ladies*. New York: Pinnacle, 1982. 265–8.

Fehler, Benedicte Ohrt. "(Re)constructing Roots: Genetics and the 'Return' of African Americans to Ghana". *Mobilities* 6.4 (2011): 585–600.

Ferguson, Kathy E., Gilad Ashkenazi and Wendy Schultz. "Gender Identity in *Star Trek*". *Political Science Fiction*. Ed. Donald M. Hassler and Clyde Wilcox. Columbia, South Carolina: U of South Carolina P, 1997. 214–33.

Fine, Cordelia. *Delusions of Gender: The Real Science Behind Sex Differences*. 2010. London: Icon, 2011.

Fischer, Claude S. *Made in America: A Social History of American Culture and Character*. Chicago: U of Chicago P, 2010.

Frye, Northrop. *Anatomy of Criticism: Four Essays*. 1957. Princeton: Princeton UP, 2000.

Fusco, Jennifer. "Marketing Insider". *Romance Writers Report*. March 2015. 42–43.

Garland Thomson, Rosemarie. *Extraordinary Bodies: Figuring Physical Disability in American Culture and Literature*. New York: Columbia UP, 1997.

Gerber, David A. "What Did Oscar Handlin Mean in the Opening Sentences of *The Uprooted?*" *Reviews in American History* 41.1 (2013): 1–11.

Gerstenzang, James and Juanita Darling. "Clinton Gives Apology for U.S. Role in Guatemala". *Los Angeles Times*. 11 March 1999. <http://articles.latimes.com/1999/mar/11/news/mn-16261>.

Goris, An. "Happily Ever After ... And After: Serialization and the Popular Romance Novel". *Americana: The Journal of American Popular Culture* 12.1 (2013). <http://www.americanpopularculture. com/journal/articles/spring_2013/goris.htm>.

Gray, Colin S. "National Style in Strategy: The American Example". *International Security* 6.2 (1981): 21–47.

Grey, Zane. *The Light of Western Stars*. New York: Grosset & Dunlap, 1914. <http://archive.org/details/cu31924012925321>.

Haddon, Jenny and Diane Pearson, eds. *Fabulous at Fifty: Recollections of the Romantic Novelists' Association 1960–2010*. N.p.: Romantic Novelists' Association, 2010.

Hague, Euan. "Mass Market Romance Fiction and the Representation of Scotland in the United States". *The Modern Scottish Diaspora: Contemporary Debates and Perspectives*. Ed. Murray Stewart Leith and Duncan Sim. Edinburgh: Edinburgh UP, 2014. 171–90.

Hague, Euan. "The Scottish Diaspora: Tartan Day and the Appropriation of Scottish Identities in the United States". *Celtic*

Geographies: Old Culture, New Times. Ed. David C. Harvey, Rhys Jones, Neil McInroy and Christine Milligan. London: Routledge, 2002. 139–56.

Hague, Euan and David Stenhouse. "A Very Interesting Place: Representing Scotland in American Romance Novels". *The Edinburgh Companion to Contemporary Scottish Literature.* Ed. Berthold Schoene. Edinburgh: Edinburgh UP, 2007. 354–61.

Handley, William R. *Marriage, Violence, and the Nation in the American Literary West.* New York: Cambridge UP, 2002.

Handlin, Oscar. *The Uprooted: The Epic Story of the Great Migrations That Made the American People.* New York: Grosset & Dunlap, 1951.

Harlequin. "Writing Guidelines: Writing American Romance". eHarlequin.com. 20 June 2007. <https://web.archive.org/web/20070620101333/http://www.eharlequin.com/articlepage.html?articleId=542&chapter=0>.

Hennegan, Alison. Introduction. *The Well of Loneliness.* By Radclyffe Hall. London: Virago, 1982. vii–xvii.

Hermes, Joke. "Sexuality in Lesbian Romance Fiction". *Feminist Review* 42 (1992): 49–66.

Hinnant, Charles H. "Desire and the Marketplace: A Reading of Kathleen Woodiwiss's *The Flame and the Flower*". *Doubled Plots: Romance and History.* Ed. Susan Strehle and Mary Paniccia Carden. Jackson: U P of Mississippi, 2003. 147–64.

Hirschman, Charles. "America's Melting Pot Reconsidered". *Annual Review of Sociology* 9 (1983): 397–423.

Hooks, Bell. *Feminism is for Everybody: Passionate Politics.* Cambridge, MA: South End, 2000.

Hume, Kathryn. *American Dream, American Nightmare: Fiction Since 1960.* Urbana: U of Illinois P, 2000.

Iannacci, Elio. "What Women Want: Gay Male Romance Novels". *The Globe and Mail.* 11 Feb. 2011. <http://www.theglobeandmail.com/life/relationships/what-women-want-gay-male-romance-novels/article565992>.

Irvin, Sherri. "Authors, Intentions and Literary Meaning". *Philosophy Compass* 1/2 (2006): 114–28.

Jacobson, Matthew Frye. *Roots Too: White Ethnic Revival in Post-Civil Rights America.* Cambridge, Massachusetts: Harvard UP, 2006.

Jacobson, Matthew Frye. *Whiteness of a Different Color: European Immigrants and the Alchemy of Race.* Cambridge, Massachusetts: Harvard UP, 1998.

Janine. "An Interview with Sharon Shinn". *Dear Author.* **9 Oct. 2006.** <http://dearauthor.com/features/interviews/an-interview-with-sharon-shinn/>.

Johnson, Allan G. *The Gender Knot: Unraveling Our Patriarchal Legacy.* 1997. Philadelphia, PA: Temple UP, 2005.

Johnson, Kevin R. "Melting Pot or Ring of Fire: Assimilation and the Mexican-American Experience". *California Law Review* 85.5 (1997): 1259–313. <http://scholarship.law.berkeley.edu/californialawreview/vol85/iss5/4>.

Joyrich, Lynne. "Feminist Enterprise? *Star Trek: The Next Generation* and the Occupation of Femininity". *Cinema Journal* 35.2 (1996): 61–84.

Juhasz, Suzanne. "Lesbian Romance Fiction and the Plotting of Desire: Narrative Theory, Lesbian Identity, and Reading Practice". *Tulsa Studies in Women's Literature* 17.1 (1998): 65–82.

Kahn, Laurie. "Jenkins on History". Popular Romance Project. n.d. Accessed 14 Oct. 2014. <http://popularromanceproject.org/wp-content/uploads/JenkinsonHistory1.pdf>.

Kallmaker, Karin. "Why Lesbian Romance?" Personal website. n.d. Accessed 6 Nov. 2013 <http://blog.kallmaker.com/p/lesbian-romance.html>.

Kamble, Jayashree. "Patriotism, Passion, and PTSD: The Critique of War in Popular Romance Fiction". *New Approaches to Popular Romance Fiction: Critical Essays.* Ed. Sarah S. G. Frantz and Eric Murphy Selinger. Jefferson, North Carolina: McFarland, 2012. 153–63.

Kamblé, Jayashree. *Making Meaning in Popular Romance Fiction: An Epistemology*. New York, NY: Palgrave Macmillan, 2014.

Kaplan, Amy. "Manifest Domesticity". *American Literature* 70.3 (1998): 581–606.

Kasperkevic, Jana. "Ben Affleck's male ancestor didn't own slaves, the female did: Report". *The Guardian*. 28 April 2015. <http://www.theguardian.com/film/2015/apr/28/ben-affleck-male-ancestor-didnt-own-slaves-the-female-did-report>.

Kay, Aaron C., John T. Jost, Anesu N. Mandisodza, Steven J. Sherman, John V. Petrocelli and Amy L. Johnson. "Panglossian Ideology in the Service of System Justification: How Complementary Stereotypes Help Us To Rationalize Inequality". *Advances in Experimental Social Psychology* 39 (2007): 305–58.

Keely, Karen. "Sexuality and Storytelling: Literary Representations of the 'Feebleminded' in the Age of Sterilization". *Mental Retardation in America: A Historical Reader*. Ed. Steven Noll and James W. Trent Jr. New York: New York UP, 2004. 207–22.

Kimmel, Michael S. *Manhood in America: A Cultural History*. 1996. New York: Oxford UP, 2006.

Kinsale, Laura. "Renegade Muse". Personal website. n.d. Accessed 12 March 2012. <http://www.laurakinsale.com/tea/detail/war/>.

Kittredge, William. *Owning it All*. Saint Paul, Minnesota: Graywolf, 1987.

Kolodny, Annette. *The Lay of the Land: Metaphor as Experience and History in American Life and Letters*. Chapel Hill: U of North Carolina P, 1975.

Krentz, Jayne Ann. Introduction. *Dangerous Men and Adventurous Women: Romance Writers on the Appeal of the Romance*. Ed. Jayne Ann Krentz. Philadelphia: U of Pennsylvania P, 1992. 1–9.

Krentz, Jayne Ann. "Why Explore Popular Romance". Vimeo. Ed. Laurie Kahn. Posted 12 December 2014. <http://vimeo.com/114372907>.

Kroes, Rob. "American Empire and Cultural Imperialism: A View from the Receiving End". *Diplomatic History* 23.3 (1999): 463–77.

L'Amour, Louis. *The Burning Hills*. 1956. New York: Bantam, 2009.

Larson, Doran. "Machine as Messiah: Cyborgs, Morphs, and the American Body Politic". *Cinema Journal* 36.4 (1997): 57–75.

Laver, Harry S. "Refuge of Manhood: Masculinity and the Militia Experience in Kentucky". *Southern Manhood: Perspectives on Masculinity in the Old South*. Ed. Craig Thompson Friend and Lorri Glover. Athens: U of Georgia P, 2004. 1–21.

Lawson, Corrina. "Science Fiction Romance: An Author's View". *Sequential Tart*. 1 Oct. 2006. <http://www.sequentialtart.com/article.php?id=279>.

Leeder, Murray. "Collective Screams: William Castle and the Gimmick Film". *Journal of Popular Culture* 44.4 (2011): 773–95.

Lennard, John and Mary Luckhurst. *The Drama Handbook: A Guide to Reading Plays*. Oxford: Oxford UP, 2002.

Lewis, Carolyn Herbst. *Prescription for Heterosexuality: Sexual Citizenship in the Cold War Era*. Chapel Hill: U of North Carolina P, 2010.

Limerick, Patricia Nelson. "What on Earth is the New Western History?" *Montana: The Magazine of Western History* 40.3 (1990): 61–4.

Linke, Gabriele. "Contemporary Mass Market Romances as National and International Culture: A Comparative Study of Mills & Boon and Harlequin Romances". *Paradoxa* 3.1–2 (1997): 195–213.

Lippi-Green, Rosina. *English with an Accent: Language, Ideology, and Discrimination in the United States*. 2nd ed. London: Routledge, 2012.

Livingston, Steven and Todd Eachus. "Indexing News After the Cold War: Reporting U.S. Ties to Latin American Paramilitary Organizations". *Political Communication* 13.4 (1996): 423–36.

Lystra, Karen. *Searching the Heart: Women, Men, and Romantic Love in Nineteenth-Century America*. 1989. New York: Oxford UP, 1992.

Malone, Michael P. "Beyond the Last Frontier: Toward a New Approach to Western American History". *The Western Historical*

Quarterly **20.4** (1989): 409–27.

Marks, Deborah. *Disability: Controversial Debates and Psychosocial Perspectives.* London: Routledge, 1999.

Martin, Joel W. "'My Grandmother Was a Cherokee Princess': Representations of Indians in Southern History". *Dressing in Feathers: The Construction of the Indian in American Popular Culture.* Ed. S. Elizabeth Bird. Boulder, Colorado: Westview, 1998. 129–47.

Maynard, Lee Anna. "LaVyrle Spencer". *Teaching American Literature: A Journal of Theory and Practice* 2.2/3 (2008).

McAdams, Dan P. "American Identity: The Redemptive Self". *The General Psychologist* 43.1 (2008): 20–7. <http://www.apadivisions. org/division-1/publications/newsletters/general/2008/04-issue. pdf>.

McAdams, Dan P. "The Redemptive Self: Generativity and the Stories Americans Live By". *Research in Human Development* 3.2–3 (2006): 81–100.

McAdams, Dan P. *The Redemptive Self: Stories Americans Live By.* New York, NY: Oxford UP, 2006.

McAleer, Joseph. *Passion's Fortune: The Story of Mills & Boon.* Oxford: Oxford UP, 1999.

McCarthy, James and Euan Hague. "Race, Nation, and Nature: The Cultural Politics of 'Celtic' Identification in the American West". *Annals of the Association of American Geographers* 94.2 (2004): 387–408.

McCracken, Scott. *Pulp: Reading Popular Fiction.* Manchester: Manchester UP, 1998.

McLeman, Robert A. "On the Origins of Environmental Migration". *Fordham Environmental Law Review* 20.2 (2009): 403–25.

McVeigh, Stephen. *The American Western.* Edinburgh: Edinburgh UP, 2007.

Menjívar, Cecilia and Néstor Rodríguez. "New Responses to State Terror". *When States Kill: Latin America, the U.S., and Technologies of Terror.* Ed. Cecilia Menjívar and Néstor Rodríguez. Austin: U of Texas P, 2005. 335–46.

Menjívar, Cecilia and Néstor Rodríguez. "State Terror in the U.S.-Latin American Interstate Regime". *When States Kill: Latin America, the U.S., and Technologies of Terror*. Ed. Cecilia Menjívar and Néstor Rodríguez. Austin: U of Texas P, 2005. 3–27.

Milan, Courtney. "Politics and the Blogging Author". 3 Sept. 2008. <http://www.courtneymilan.com/ramblings/2008/09/03/politics-and-the-blogging-author/>.

Moffatt, Laurie Norton. "The People's Painter". *Norman Rockwell: Pictures for the American People*. Ed. Maureen Hart Hennessey and Anne Knutson. New York: Harry N. Abrams, 1999. 23–7.

Morsi, Pamela. "Sarah Palin's kick in the gut". 21 Feb. 2010. <http://pamelamorsi.blogspot.co.uk/2010/02/sarah-palins-kick-in-gut.html>.

Morsi, Pamela. "The Story Behind SIMPLE JESS". 12 Jan. 2015. <http://www.pamelamorsi.com/?p=251>.

Murray, Stuart and James McCabe. *Norman Rockwell's "Four Freedoms": Images that Inspire a Nation*. Stockbridge, MA: Berkshire House and The Norman Rockwell Museum, 1993.

Mussell, Kay. Introduction. *North American Romance Writers*. Ed. Kay Mussell and Johanna Tuñón. Lanham, Maryland: Scarecrow, 1999. 1–9.

Nachbar, Jack and Kevin Lause. "Songs of the Unseen Road: Myths, Beliefs and Values in Popular Culture". *Popular Culture: An Introductory Text*. Ed. Jack Nachbar and Kevin Lause. Bowling Green, OH: Bowling Green State U Popular P, 1992. 82–109.

Neal, Lynn. S. *Romancing God: Evangelical Women and Inspirational Fiction*. Chapel Hill: U of North Carolina P, 2006.

Novak, Michael. *Unmeltable Ethnics: Politics & Culture in American Life*. 2nd ed. New Brunswick, New Jersey: Transaction Publishers, 1996.

Osborne, Gwendolyn E. "In Search of Women Who Look Like Me: A Brief History of the African-American Romance". *The 2000–2003 Proceedings of the SW/Texas PCA/ACA Conference*, Ed. Leslie

Fife. 2003. 2020–44.

Ostrov Weisser, Susan. *The Glass Slipper: Women and Love Stories.* New Brunswick, NJ: Rutgers UP, 2013.

Palmer, Paulina. "Girl Meets Girl: Changing Approaches to the Lesbian Romance". *Fatal Attractions: Re-scripting Romance in Contemporary Literature and Film.* Ed. Lynne Pearce and Gina Wisker. London: Pluto, 1998. 189–204.

Plant, E. Ashby and B. Michelle Peruche. "The Consequences of Race for Police Officers' Responses to Criminal Suspects". *Psychological Science* 16.3 (2005): 180–3. <https://www.psychologicalscience.org/pdf/ps/racialbias.pdf>.

Putnam, Robert D. *Bowling Alone: The Collapse and Revival of American Community.* New York: Simon & Schuster, 2000.

Raboteau, Albert J. "African Americans, Exodus, and the American Israel". *Religion and American Culture: A Reader.* Ed. David G. Hackett. 2nd ed. New York: Routledge, 2003. 75–87.

Radner, Hilary. *Shopping Around: Feminine Culture and the Pursuit of Pleasure.* New York: Routledge, 1995.

Radway, Janice A. *Reading the Romance: Women, Patriarchy, and Popular Literature.* 1984. Chapel Hill: U of North Carolina P, 1991.

Ramsdell, Kristin. *Romance Fiction: A Guide to the Genre.* 2nd ed. Santa Barbara, California: Libraries Unlimited, 2012.

Ray, Celeste. "Scottish Heritage Southern Style". *Southern Cultures* 4.2 (1998): 28–45.

Reagan, Michael. *In the Words of Ronald Reagan: The Wit, Wisdom, and Eternal Optimism of America's 40th President.* Nashville, Tennessee: Thomas Nelson, 2004.

Regis, Pamela. *A Natural History of the Romance Novel.* Philadelphia, Pennsylvania: U of Pennsylvania P, 2003.

Regis, Pamela. "Female Genre Fiction in the Twentieth Century". *The Cambridge History of the American Novel.* Ed. Leonard Cassuto, Clare Virginia Eby and Benjamin Reiss. Cambridge: Cambridge UP, 2011. 847–60.

Richards, Penny L. " 'Beside Her Sat Her Idiot Child': Families and Developmental Disability in Mid-Nineteenth-Century America". *Mental Retardation in America: A Historical Reader*. Ed. Steven Noll and James W. Trent Jr. New York: New York UP, 2004. 65–84.

Roach, Catherine. "Getting a Good Man to Love: Popular Romance Fiction and the Problem of Patriarchy". *Journal of Popular Romance Studies* 1.1 (2010). <http://jprstudies.org/2010/08/getting-a-good-man-to-love-popular-romance-fiction-and-the-problem-of-patriarchy-by-catherine-roach/>.

Rockwell, Norman. *My Adventures as an Illustrator.* New York: Harry N. Abrams, 1988.

Rodgers, Daniel T. *The Work Ethic in Industrial America 1850–1920.* 1974. Chicago: U of Chicago P, 1979.

Romance Writers of America. "About the Romance Genre". n.d. Accessed 24 Dec. 2014 <http://my.rwa.org/romance>.

Roosevelt, Franklin D. "Message to Congress 1941". Franklin D. Roosevelt Presidential Library and Museum. <http://www.fdrlibrary.marist.edu/pdfs/ffreadingcopy.pdf>.

Rose, Sarah Frances. *No Right to be Idle: The Invention of Disability, 1850–1930.* Ph.D. thesis. Chicago, Illinois: U of Illinois at Chicago, 2008.

Rosenwein, Barbara H. "Worrying About Emotions in History". *The American Historical Review* 107.3 (2002): 821–45.

Rotundo, E. Anthony. "Body and Soul: Changing Ideals of American Middle-Class Manhood, 1770–1920". *Journal of Social History* 16.4 (1983): 23–38.

Roulo, Claudette. "Defense Department Expands Women's Combat Role". U.S. Department of Defense. 24 Jan. 2013. <http://archive.defense.gov/news/newsarticle.aspx?id=119098>.

Rowland, Robert C. and John M. Jones. "Recasting the American Dream and American Politics: Barack Obama's Keynote Address to the 2004 Democratic National Convention". *Quarterly Journal of Speech* 93.4 (2007): 425–48.

Ryley, John. *The Leeds Guide; Including a Sketch of the Environs, and Kirkstall Abbey*. Leeds: Edward Baines, 1806. <http://archive.org/details/leedsguideinclu00rylegoog>.

Satterwhite, Emily. "'That's What They're All Singing About': Appalachian Heritage, Celtic Pride, and American Nationalism at the 2003 Smithsonian Folklife Festival". *Appalachian Journal* 32.3 (2005): 302–38.

Schafer, Susanne M. "1st Female Fighter Pilot Tapped as Wing Commander". Associated Press. 31 May 2012. <http://bigstory.ap.org/content/1st-female-fighter-pilot-tapped-wing-commander>.

Scheper-Hughes, Nancy, and Margaret M. Lock. "The Mindful Body: A Prolegomenon to Future Work in Medical Anthropology". *Medical Anthropology Quarterly* ns 1.1 (1987): 6–41.

Schuster, Marilyn R. "Strategies for Survival: The Subtle Subversion of Jane Rule". *Feminist Studies* 7.3 (1981): 431–50.

Shinn, Sharon. "Twelve Houses Series". Personal website. n.d. Accessed 29 June 2014. <http://sharonshinn.net/HTML/twelvehouse.html>.

Shklar, Judith N. *American Citizenship: The Quest for Inclusion*. 1991. Cambridge, Massachusetts: Harvard UP, 1995.

Sim, Duncan. *American Scots: The Scottish Diaspora and the USA*. Edinburgh: Dunedin Academic P, 2011.

Sinclair, Linnea. "Debunking Authorly Urban Legends". *Alien Romances*. 27 Nov. 2006. <http://aliendjinnromances.blogspot.co.uk/2006/11/debunking-authorly-urban-legends.html>.

Sinclair, Linnea. "Facts, Games of Command and the Wizard of Oz". Email to the author. 29 May 2012.

Sinclair, Linnea. "Facts, Games of Command and the Wizard of Oz". Email to the author. 30 May 2012.

Sinclair, Linnea. "The Admiral Answers, Part 1". *Alien Romances*. 24 Sept. 2007. <http://aliendjinnromances.blogspot.co.uk/2007/09/admiral-answers-part-1.html>.

Skerry, Philip and Brenda Berstler. "You Are What You Wear: The

Role of Western Costume in Film". *Beyond the Stars III: The Material World in American Popular Film.* Ed. Paul Loukides and Linda K. Fuller. Bowling Green, OH: Bowling Green State U Popular P, 1993. 77–86.

Slotkin, Richard. *Gunfighter Nation: The Myth of the Frontier in Twentieth-Century America.* 1992. New York: HarperPerennial, 1993.

Smoak, Gregory E. "Beyond the Academy: Making the New Western History Matter in Local Communities". *The Public Historian* 31.4 (2009): 85–9.

Sommer, Doris. *Foundational Fictions: The National Romances of Latin America.* 1991. Berkeley: U of California P, 1993.

Spurgeon, Sara L. *Exploding the Western: Myths of Empire on the Postmodern Frontier.* College Station: Texas A & M UP, 2005.

Squires, Judith. "Politics Beyond Boundaries: A Feminist Perspective". *What is Politics?: The Activity and its Study.* Ed. Adrian Leftwich. Cambridge, UK: Polity, 2004. 119–34.

Staub, Ervin. *The Roots of Evil: The Origins of Genocide and Other Group Violence.* 1989. Cambridge: Cambridge UP, 1992.

Stefoff, Rebecca. *Robots.* Tarrytown, NY: Marshall Cavendish Benchmark, 2008.

Stoneley, Peter. "'Never Love a Cowboy': Romance Fiction and Fantasy Families". *Writing and Fantasy.* Ed. Ceri Sullivan and Barbara White. London: Longman, 1999. 223–35.

Stott, Richard. "British Immigrants and the American 'Work Ethic' in the Mid-Nineteenth-Century". *Labor History* 26.1 (1985): 86–102.

Tasker, Yvonne. "Soldiers' Stories: Women and Military Masculinities in *Courage Under Fire*". *Quarterly Review of Film and Video* 19.3 (2002): 209–22.

Thompson, Gerald. "Another Look at Frontier versus Western Historiography". *Montana: The Magazine of Western History* 40.3 (1990): 68–71.

Tompkins, Jane. *West of Everything: The Inner Life of Westerns.*

1992. New York: Oxford UP, 1993.

Tourism Intelligence Scotland. *Ancestral Tourism in Scotland*. 2013. <www.scottish-enterprise.com/~/media/se_2013/knowledge%20 hub/publication/11%20ancestral%20tourism.pdf>.

Trent, James W. Jr. *Inventing the Feeble Mind: A History of Mental Retardation in the United States*. Berkeley, California: U of California P, 1994.

Tuveson, Ernest Lee. *Redeemer Nation: The Idea of America's Millennial Role*. Chicago: U of Chicago P, 1968.

Vivanco, Laura. *For Love and Money: The Literary Art of the Harlequin Mills & Boon Romance*. Tirril, Penrith: Humanities-Ebooks, 2011.

Washington, George. "From General Washington: Mount Vernon, July 25, 1785". *Memoirs, Correspondence and Manuscripts of General Lafayette*, vol. 2. London: Saunders and Otley, 1837. 114–18. <http://books.google.co.uk/books?id=RDB66nh0t2gC& printsec=frontcover#v=onepage&q&f=false>.

Waters, Mary C. *Ethnic Options: Choosing Identities in America*. Berkeley: U of California P, 1990.

Weir, Robert E. *Beyond Labor's Veil: The Culture of the Knights of Labor*. University Park, PA: Pennsylvania State UP, 1996.

Weiss, Dennis M. "*Star Trek* and the Posthuman". Personal webpages. n.d. Accessed 3 June 2012. <http://faculty.ycp.edu/~dweiss/ research/Star%20Trek%20and%20the%20Posthuman.pdf>.

Wendell, Sarah. *Everything I Know About Love I Learned from Romance Novels*. Naperville, Illinois: Sourcebooks Casablanca, 2011.

Westbrook, Robert B. "Fighting for the American Family: Private Interests and Political Obligation in World War II". *The Power of Culture: Critical Essays in American History*. Ed. Richard Wightman Fox & T. J. Jackson Lears. Chicago: U of Chicago P, 1993. 195–221.

Wilkinson, Richard and Kate Pickett. *The Spirit Level: Why Equality is Better for Everyone*. London: Penguin, 2010.

Williamson, Penelope. "By Honor Bound: The Heroine as Hero". *Dangerous Men and Adventurous Women: Romance Writers on the Appeal of the Romance*. Ed. Jayne Ann Krentz. Philadelphia: U of Pennsylvania P, 1992. 125–32.

Wister, Owen. *The Virginian*. 1902. Ed. Robert Shulman. Oxford: Oxford UP, 1998.

Worster, Donald. "Beyond the Agrarian Myth". *Trails: Toward a New Western History*. Ed. Patricia Nelson Limerick, Clyde A. Milner II and Charles E. Rankin. Lawrence, Kansas: UP of Kansas, 1991. 3–25.

Young, Erin S. "Escaping the 'Time Bind': Negotiations of Love and Work in Jayne Ann Krentz's 'Corporate Romances'". *Journal of American Culture* 33.2 (2010): 92–106.

A Note on the Author

LAURA VIVANCO is an independent scholar of romance fiction, including both modern popular romance and mediaeval Hispanic literature. She has a PhD from the University of St Andrews, and is the author of *Death in Fifteenth-Century Castile: Ideologies of the Elites* (Woodbridge: Tamesis, 2004) and *For Love and Money: The Literary Art of the Harlequin Mills & Boon Romance* (Humanities-Ebooks, 2011). She is a member of the International Association for the Study of Popular Romance and a regular contributor to Teach Me Tonight (http://teachmetonight.blogspot.com/) an academic blog devoted to the study of popular romance novels.

Humanities-Ebooks.co.uk

All Humanities Ebooks titles are available to Libraries in PDF through Ebrary, EBSCO and MyiLibrary.com

Sibylle Baumbach, *Shakespeare and the Art of Physiognomy**
John Beer, *Blake's Humanism*
John Beer, *The Achievement of E M Forster*
John Beer, *Coleridge the Visionary*
Jared Curtis, ed., *The Fenwick Notes of William Wordsworth**
Jared Curtis, ed., *The Cornell Wordsworth: A Supplement**
ared Curtis, ed., *The Poems of William Wordsworth: Collected Reading Texts from the Cornell Wordsworth*, 3 vols.
Steven Duncan, *Analytic Philosophy of Religion: its History since 1955**
Richard Gravil, *Wordsworth and Helen Maria Williams; or, the Perils of Sensibility*
Richard Gravil, *Romantic Dialogues: Anglo-American Continuities, 1776–1862 **
John K Hale, *Milton as Multilingual: Selected Essays 1982–2004*
Simon Hull, ed., *The British Periodical Text, 1797–1835*
Rob Johnson, Mark Levene and Penny Roberts, eds., *History at the End of the World **
John Lennard, *Modern Dragons and other Essays on Genre Fiction**
John Lennard, *Of Sex and Faerie: Further Essays on Genre Fiction**
C W R D Moseley, *Shakespeare's History Plays**
Colin Nicholson, *Fivefathers: Interviews with late Twentieth-Century Scottish Poets*
W J B Owen and J W Smyser, eds., *Wordsworth's Political Writings**
Pamela Perkins, ed., *Francis Jeffrey's Highland and Continental Tours**
Keith Sagar, *D. H. Lawrence: Poet**
Reinaldo Francisco Silva, *Portuguese American Literature**
Laura Vivanco, *For Love and Money: the Harlequin Mills & Boom Romance**
William Wordsworth, *Concerning the Convention of Cintra**

* These titles are also available in print using links from
http://www.humanities-ebooks.co.uk

Made in the USA
San Bernardino, CA
05 February 2017